Sew the Heart

Sue Batton Leonard

Published 2016.
Printed in the United States of America.

ISBN 978-1-943659-34-7

Library of Congress Control Number 2016953713

This book was published by BookCrafters,
Parker, Colorado.
www.bookcrafters.net
This book may be ordered from
www.bookcrafters.net and other online bookstores.

I dedicate this book to all women I have crossed paths with during this journey called life. Thank you for your friendship, love, inspiration and mentorship.

All characters are a compilation of personalities of women I have known throughout my lifetime. Even if I don't know you, perhaps you may recognize a bit of yourself in the story.

Chapter 1

"I've had it," Moxie said out loud to herself, wiping the tears from her eyes with the arm of her black long sleeve tee-shirt. Pitch black mascara ran from her eyes all over her cheeks. She had no idea how long she had been walking along the leaf-covered railroad tracks. Stopping several times that morning, she sat between the rails, inert, unable to move ahead, lost in thought.

Every day for the past few months, she walked a portion of the railroad tracks from where she lived far outside the southern Colorado town of Kellenville to her part-time job at a donut shop in Hopewell. As the crow flies she lived closer to Hopewell.

With each step one more bad memory was stirred up. Although each mile along the railroad tracks held exquisite views of the Sangre de Cristo Mountains, with fourteen thousand foot peaks, she couldn't find any beauty in her surroundings. She was too despondent. It was as if the girl was walking between rows of tall cornstalks on flat fields, without the ability to see out. With each step it was as if she went deeper into a dark tunnel. Memories replayed of relationships gone wrong, the teasing she had endured all her life, the insecure feelings she'd had when she realized her life was so different and empty compared to some of her school mates. Although lots of friends came from broken households, she wondered why none of her friends were screwed up like her. And then there was her buddy Alexis who was bounced around to different foster homes just as much, but Alexis didn't seem to have any trouble handling it. She aced everything and went off to college on scholarship money.

Moxie recalled each time she was moved from foster home to foster home. Once, after four years when she was settled into a loving environment that looked like it might become permanent, it had come to naught. Again she was uprooted when "the household circumstances changed" and her foster parents decided not to adopt her. There were so many changes in "household circumstances" throughout her lifetime, she wasn't even sure how old she was when she was moved from the southeastern part of the country to the Sangre de Christo Mountains in Colorado.

All she knew for sure was she hated her life and wanted to end it. If the train barreled down the track, she'd let it sweep her under. All the pain would be gone and she wouldn't have to deal with having to support herself. Now an adult, she was really on her own and every false sense of belonging to a family was gone. She never felt more alone in her life.

I don't even know how to support myself, Moxie thought as she kicked the leaves covering the tracks with her worn shoes with soles which had begun to separate between the layers. She felt like she had been on her own trying to fend for herself ever since she was a small child. She'd gotten so little support from anyone who was supposed to be her guardian. Even her "friends" had abandoned her as she'd moved from place to place. Only thing she had to be thankful for was meeting the old lady with the donuts, Miss Eunice, who was nice enough to let her live in her one room studio apartment in her guest house. For the time being, anyway. Even if the place was out in the boonies and not near public transportation, at least she wasn't living on the streets anymore.

Moxie squatted down in the dried aspen leaves and circled her arms around her head, grabbing both elbows with her hands as if she was trying form a protective orb or cocoon around herself. She inhaled the earthy odors of the fall season and thought how she'd like to dig a hole and bury herself. She lost her balance and just as she was about to keel over from her squatting position, she caught herself with her right hand as she placed it on the ground in the pile of crunchy leaves. She swept the leaves aside and when she did, she saw something gleaming. Although it was dawn and the sun was a few minutes from rising, the contrast between her black fingernail polish and the shiny object caught her attention. At first she thought the shiny object was part of the rail, but she realized it moved when she touched it. What was a silver-colored charm bracelet doing between the railroad ties?

Moxie picked up the bracelet, and as she did a small silver cross fell off. She knew where she was headed—to the pawn place as soon as her shift ended at the donut shop.

She stood and hurried along, not taking time to really look at the jewelry. She stuffed the bracelet and the unattached charm into the pocket of her drab olive corduroy jacket that was so old, there wasn't any nap left to it. She stepped up her pace so she wouldn't be late because she couldn't risk being fired. All she had was the little money she made at the donut shop. How Moxie hated putting on the foolish pink and white uniform which made her feel ridiculous like a Miss Goody Two Shoes. She couldn't expect any hot-to-trot man to look at her twice dressed like that.

Chapter 2

Moxie finished wiping the spilled coffee off the counter and looked at the clock. Her shift was almost over. Then she remembered her plan to head right over to the pawn shop with the charm bracelet. She hoped selling it off would put a few extra dollars in her pocket.

As she took off her uniform in the employee restroom she thought how grateful she was she didn't have to launder it. It was hard to do laundry in a sink in a two room apartment. As she donned her corduroy jacket she felt for the jewelry in her pocket. She was glad she was in a spot where she could get a second look at the charm bracelet where no one else could see it before she sold it.

The bracelet was kind of interesting. Moxie wondered whether it was real silver. Sterling silver, she remembered her foster mother calling it. She thought back to when she was young and stood on a stool by the kitchen sink watching or helping her guardian polish the "sterling flatware" and her collection of serving pieces. As they worked, her foster mother pointed out the beautiful "patina" on her silver tea set which came with a large fancy tray. She often remarked she hoped Moxie would age to a rich patina with strong character. Back then she was too young to understand, but now she was old enough to know she was not headed anywhere near that direction. Not even close. Not with the way her life was going.

The failed adoption by her "sterling silver" foster mother meant leaving what she thought was going to be her "forever home," and it hurt very deeply. All of her troubles would have never happened and she'd be living a good life if the adoption had gone through. To a young child, the woman seemed to have everything a person could ever want including money, and lots of it. Moxie remembered the lady had a way about her that was kind of fun and humorous. She couldn't explain the woman, especially when she got going on one of her talking jags about the mysterious things known to have happened in the Sangre de Cristo Mountains. Living with her from age five to nine, there was a lot the woman talked about she didn't get. And so much had happened, her memories of what the woman looked like were vague and getting even more dim with the passage of time.

As an adult, Moxie felt resentment and anger brew inside her, nearly to the boiling point. Didn't Child Protective Services understand never giving a child an explanation for each move in and out of foster homes meant her feelings of rejection were intensified? She felt like a kid no one wanted, not even her birth mother.

Moxie twirled the bracelet looking at all the charms. It appeared whoever owned the bracelet had led an enchanted life. The more she looked at the baubles, the more she became curious about the owner and the significance of each item. She decided to wait until the next day to go to the pawn shop so she'd have a little more time to look at each charm. She stuffed the bracelet back into the pocket of her jacket, and began the long walk, down the railroad tracks toward "home."

Chapter 3

THE ONLY CONNECTION MOXIE FELT SHE HAD with the world was through her cell phone and computer. Some days as she walked the tracks she'd stand and cry out, Hello World, here I am. *Does anyone even care I even exist? Of course they didn't,* she thought, which added to her feelings of gut wrenching desperation and loneliness.

Thank God she was living where there was free and reliable internet access. It was surprising Miss Eunice had WiFi. After all, she was as ancient as a dinosaur. So old it made the young woman wonder who came first, the dinosaurs or Miss Eunice. The elderly woman looked as if she had weathered some tough stuff in her life, one couldn't help but notice. The only reason the old lady had WiFi was she recently upgraded her TV to a digital flat screen and had no choice if she wanted to get TV reception.

When they'd had the discussion about internet service the day Moxie moved into the guest quarters, she asked Miss Eunice what kind of computer she had. All she could say was hers was no longer functioning and it was a TRS-80 from the Tandy Corporation which the young woman figured was an acronym for the Tyrannosaurus era.

Moxie sat at the small red oval-shaped kitchenette-sized table, with a laminate top edged in chrome, and logged onto her lap-top computer. Every day was a long day between walking to work, putting in six hours and then walking home again. A peanut butter and jelly sandwich on stale bread was dinner, and she had a bag of leftover donuts from the shop. "Yum," she said sarcastically trying to convince herself more donuts were better than no food at all.

Searching for a new job should have been her priority; Moxie knew it. But it was the last thing she felt like doing. The donut shop was not exactly her idea of a great place to work. The place would have been better off if someone torched it. The booths and the stools at the counter were covered in red pleather. Any amount of scrubbing couldn't remove the film of grease that had settled on the surfaces. And the cracked linoleum floor was ancient. The only way Moxie knew the term pleather was from her foster mother, the one who had very little food in the refrigerator and lived on what seemed like her last dollar. She thought back to the joy her foster mother had when she was able to reupholster their heavily soiled couch when her husband got a raise. The yardage came from a store about to go defunct. They sold the last bolt of the latest, greatest new fabric called pleather, left over from the 1970s, at a real bargain.

Moxie often wondered how the donut shop had gotten away with not having a decent exhaust system. Perhaps they had fallen through the cracks when it came to health and safety inspections. She was getting awfully tired of smelling like greasy donuts. Sometimes by the end of her shift, she felt like gagging.

Moxie scrolled through the listings of Yard Sales and Apartments for Rent on Craigslist. She was surprised not to see her own name under the free, give-away animal postings. That's about how low she felt. She stumbled upon the Lost and Found section. Oh, how she wished she could lose her life and find another. Maybe, she thought, tomorrow her timing would be perfect. Her eye was drawn to a listing that simply stated, "Bracelet lost near Kellenville. Call 979-452-9099 to claim your reward if you have found it."

"Could it be?" Moxie wondered. "Just my poor luck, probably not."

As Moxie prepared to go to bed she decided the next day she'd try to brave it and stop by the pawn shop to see what they'd give her for the bracelet. Then, she thought, she'd know its value and who had the top offer—the pawn shop or the owner's reward. Was it even the one posted on Craigslist? She went over to the computer and reread the posting. The reward amount was not disclosed, and the details of the bracelet were non-descript.

A bronze colored lighthouse, a knotted rope, a church with a small red door, a miniature baby's shoe, a teardrop pearl, a ship that looked like a cruise liner were just some of the miniature baubles Moxie studied. She sat looking over the bracelet pondering whether she even had the guts to take it to the pawn dealer. Maybe, she thought, she'd call the phone number on Craigslist tomorrow.

If only she knew what to do. She placed the bracelet on the table next to the saggy futon and slipped under the covers. Her last thoughts before drifting off to sleep were of finding the best option for putting a large chunk of money in her pocket.

Chapter 4

MOXIE WOKE WITH A START after a very restless night. Between thinking about the bracelet and her growling stomach, she tossed and turned for hours. In the wee hours of the morning, she finally fell into a deep sleep.

When she woke she realized if she didn't hurry, she'd be late for work. She walked the tracks quicker than ever before. Things seemed a little less pathetic that morning since she had what might be a big ticket item in her possession.

As she came in through the back door to the donut shop her boss Matthew greeted her cheerfully, looking bright-eyed and full of energy. "Good morning, Moxie. How was your trek in? Did you see anything different along the way?"

"Like what?" Moxie responded with a grouchy tone in her voice.

"I don't know. Something life-changing?" Matthew found when he walked, it gave him time to think and he was able to solve all kinds of problems. He enjoyed looking at the beauty of nature.

Did Matthew know something about what she had found on the track? Moxie wondered. She was beginning to feel a little paranoid and anxious about the bracelet. Perhaps, she thought, she'd best be rid of it quickly. When she thought about entering a pawn shop again, she could feel her pulse quickening and thrumming in her ears.

"Hello!" a man with a friendly voice said from behind the pawn shop counter as Moxie entered. The door behind her blew and slammed shut. She jumped.

"Cold out there today, isn't it? Looks like snow."

"Kinda," Moxie said tersely. She couldn't handle making small talk. She was on a mission trying to figure out how you approach a pawn dealer to sell something. The one and only other time she'd been in a pawn shop was when she was fourteen years old, nine years ago, when her mission was very different. Her twenty-one year old foster brother, Jared, had promised if she'd be his partner-in-crime, he'd get her the tattoo she so badly wanted, and pay for it.

"Here's the deal," Jared said, "you help me pull this off, babe, and the hottest dudes in Kellenville will be like... knocking at your door and more."

"Screw being the good girl, let's do it, Jared," thinking of the tattoo in her future, and the guys lining up to do her. She couldn't wait to experience what her friends had been talking about. They made sex sound so exciting and she couldn't wait to get in on the action. It was hard to join in on some conversations with her girlfriends since she was still "clean and untarnished" as her foster mother called being a virgin ever so politely.

"Let me ask you," said Jared. "How can we fail? It's an easy score. The Ultimate Pawn's valuables aren't even locked up in a case."

"What if there are like... security cameras?" asked Moxie.

"Don't worry about it! I've got the place scoped. There aren't any. The place looks like it barely ekes by. I'm sure they don't have money for an alarm system and security cameras. The pawn shops in Kellenville are lame. They aren't well outfitted like they are in Hopewell," Jared assured her.

Like any sister does with her big brother, she looked up to Jared. She had to admit to herself the fact that Jared had asked her to get in on his plans was kind of flattering. The thought of finally getting a tattoo was enticing.

She could only imagine how her friends would react when they found out she had the guts to go through with a theft. They couldn't believe how easy Jared made pulling things like that off. "After all he is a charmer," they all said, "and he like... never gets caught."

Many years later, Moxie wondered if she would have let her foster brother use her as an accomplice if she hadn't been stoned out of her mind.

The partners-in-crime were successful in

shoplifting two pairs of diamond earrings. Afterward they celebrated by going to the Tattoo Place and having their "score" date etched on their necks and wrists. Not such a bright idea as it turned out. It became her first brush with the law. The tattoo artist, who was also a nark, called the cops after he finished their jobs. They had openly discussed their thrilling day and what they would do differently next time. Fortunately she was a minor and determined to only be an accomplice. Things turned out differently for her twenty-one year old foster brother. Although, Jared said his sentence was better than having to return home and face more years of living with an abusive father.

Moxie walked from counter to counter and from shelf to shelf looking at the items avoiding the eyes of the shopkeeper. *Oh, God,* she thought. She sure hoped the storekeeper wasn't going to ask questions about where she got the bracelet. She played out various conversations in her head as she tried to warm her cold feet and hands.

Moving toward the clear glass counter where the pawn dealer was standing, Moxie lingered looking down at the merchandise. Realizing she was the only one in the shop, she thought, *It's now or never.*

"I have a bracelet," she said to the man behind the counter "and I am wondering how much you'll give me for it."

"Let's see it," the man said. She handed the dealer the jewelry. Her hands were shaking, and she had broken into a cold sweat. Her eyes stared down at the glass top counter in front of her checking out what items were on display in the jewelry section. She couldn't help but notice the secure lock on the cabinetry. Really, it was no one's fault other than their own, she and Jared robbed the Ultimate Pawn since they didn't even have their valuables securely locked away in a display cabinet. *How stupid was that?* Moxie thought, justifying what she had done nine years prior.

"Just a few," the pawn shop dealer said.

Did he mean he'll give me like...a few dollars? Moxie wondered. She understood what he meant when she looked up and saw he was studying the jewelry with a magnifying device. Obviously the storekeeper needed a few minutes to determine its value by the way he was looking so closely at the chain and at each bauble on the bracelet.

"Seventy-five dollars," the dealer said, sounding final.

"Seventy-five? I'll have to think about it."

The clerk handed the bracelet back. "Good luck trying to get more than what I am offering you. It's a very fair deal."

Moxie had no idea whether the man was trying to pull a fast one or not; it was so hard to trust a soul. Before selling it off she decided she'd find out more about the reward being offered on Craigslist.

Chapter 5

It seemed like she had just paid her cellphone bill, and now it was coming due again. It was already the twentieth of the month and Moxie had four more days to get her act together and scrape up the money. Did it really matter if she lost communication with the world? She had no mother or father, sisters or brothers or friends. As if anyone really cared if she disappeared off the face of the earth. Her boss Matthew was nice enough, and then there was Miss Eunice. The only time she really heard from her was when Miss Eunice needed to have someone enter the apartment to check the "electrics," as she called it. Moxie wondered whether she ought to let the cellphone go and close out her account. It would be one less thing to worry about paying for in the no-good life of hers.

She sighed deeply, picked up her cellphone and dialed 979-452-9099. After a few rings, and what sounded like a lot of fumbling, a man answered the phone. "Hello," a voice said abruptly.

Moxie considered hanging up. "Hello," she said, her voice barely audible. I am calling about the listing I saw on Craigslist in the Lost and Found section."

"Oh," said the man on the other end of the phone, "you'll have to deal with my mother on that one. I posted the blurb on Craigslist for her but she'll have to call you back. But before I take your phone number, we need to establish if you found the right piece of jewelry...my mother's. Can you tell me some of the details? Where you found it?"

"Yeah, I found it along the railroad tracks, on the outskirts of Kellenville headed towards Hopewell."

"On the railroad tracks? What does it look like?"

Moxie swallowed hard. "What does what look like?" She didn't know if he meant the place where she found the bracelet along the tracks or the bracelet itself.

"Wait a minute, let me go get it." Her life was so messed up; everything was wacked out, even her memory. She had a hard time focusing on anything, and she couldn't remember small details like the charms on the bracelet she had found a week ago. She crossed the small room to grab the bracelet off the table next to the futon, where she had last put it. There was nothing there other than a glass of week old water. Where was it?

"I can't find the bracelet right now," she said, returning to the phone. "Hold on, let me look under the furniture. Maybe it fell off the table." She saw nothing but a few cobwebs and dust bunnies.

"Come on, stop wasting my time," said the man gruffly and impatiently, "if you can't give me the most distinguishing feature on the bracelet, I have a hard time believing it is the same one that was lost." He sounded like a stereotypical bully. A vision of a short, stocky, burly guy crossed her mind. Moxie was well-acquainted with the type from the year she spent in the foster home with the abusive man. Even the children who were his natural born, she heard years later when she was in her late teens, had to be eventually removed from the home. When a neighbor saw him slapping around his wife big time, she called Child Protective Services. That got the ball rolling for removing his children out of the household, Jared's siblings.

Moxie wracked her brain trying to remember the details of the bracelet. Hearing a voice that sounded like one from the past pushed something heavy through her stomach, and she couldn't think straight.

"All I can remember is it had like… a lot of charms on it," Moxie said.

"Now we're getting someplace," the man said. "Give me your number and I'll have my mother call you back."

"Okay, how much is the reward anyway?"

"Like I said, you'll have to deal with my mother. Give me your number. She'll call you back."

"When will that be? Like… today?" Moxie asked anxiously. She needed the reward money. And quickly. She gave out her phone number and hung up.

"Darn it," she said out loud. Where had she put the bracelet? She wanted to use the most shocking swear words she could think of, but a little nagging voice in the back of her mind reminded her of what her sterling silver foster mother always said about curse words. "There is no point in cussing. It won't do anything to correct the circumstances, it only agitates further. There is no point in using them."

She checked for the tenth time in the pockets of her corduroy jacket she wore back and forth to work, even though she knew it was a wasted effort. She was sure she had left the bracelet on the table. Her "big ticket item" was lost and it was just one more instance nothing in her life went right. She unfolded the futon and felt along the crease where the furniture folded in half. Nothing.

Moxie stopped suddenly when she remembered a few days ago when she returned home from work she found her door unlocked. That day, just like every day, she had locked it. Hadn't she?

Why did she ever lock the door anyway? What was it she had anyone would want to steal? All her worldly possessions fit into a large duffel bag. There was nothing of value—just clothes she purchased at the thrift shop. Although, some of them were kind of cute, she thought.

She turned out the light and climbed into bed. The stress of hearing the brusque voice on the phone had worn her out. And even more tiring was walking the tracks nearly every day on a rather meager diet. She needed to find some other way to get back and forth to work. She drifted off to sleep dreaming of the day when the "big ticket item" was going to change her life.

Chapter 6

"BIG TICKET ITEM?" Moxie asked herself, the moment she woke up. "What was I thinking?" The moment she opened her eyes she remembered she couldn't find the big ticket item. Well, forget getting a reward payment or money at the pawn shop. She should have taken up the pawn dealer's offer, right then and there the other day. She'd have had seventy-five bucks in her pocket. Moxie quickly dressed, ran out the door, and started down the tracks toward work.

"Good morning Moxie," Matthew said when he turned around from the coffee machine he was filling with water. "What's new with you today?" Not a damn thing, Moxie felt like saying but instead she shrugged her shoulders. How could Matthew be so happy every morning working at the grease pit frying up donuts?

"What's new with me?" Moxie reiterated Matthew's question in her mind. She had decided on her next day off, she was going to sit on the tracks and just wait for the train to plow her down. She'd sit there all day if she had to. She hadn't yet figured out the train's schedule, and she was more distraught than ever. The woman who was going to call back about the charm bracelet, hadn't. Not that it mattered. She still hadn't found the bracelet. She'd torn the tiny apartment apart one more time in hopes of finding the bracelet and had come up empty handed. What was the use of living if you were nothing but a loser? Not a frickin' thing ever went right. She knew when she thought like that she sounded like her foster mother, the one who got slapped around by the husband. But it was true. Not a frickin' thing ever did go right. And she thought mockingly, she sure as hell was not turning into a person with a rich patina.

The bell tinkled at the front door of the coffee shop, and Moxie turned around to see if she needed to seat anybody or whether the customer was getting in line for coffee and donuts to go. She only had a few more minutes left of her shift and oh how she hoped it was not going to be a table full of people. She needed any extra tips she could get, but she had very little patience that morning. She just wanted to get off her shift, go home and bury her head or even better be run over by the train. Just when she thought things may have begun to go right with finding the bracelet, "her big ticket item," it all came crashing down once again. She'd lost the thing. How could that have happened?

"Yoo-hoo! Hi neighbor," Moxie heard the familiar voice. She turned to see who the customer was calling out to and saw it was Miss Eunice. She went over to table and wiped it down with her rag, and put a napkin, a spoon and a cup in front of her landlady and filled the mug with steaming hot coffee.

"Mornin' Miss Eunice, what would you like?" she asked in a flat, monotone voice.

"Just a cup of coffee this morning and before I go, I'll take your daily deal, the donuts leftover when you close. Hope you have some chocolate ones this morning." Moxie was not completely surprised to see her landlady. She frequented the place quite often especially right before closing and liked the deals the donut shop owner offered at the end of the day. She'd buy a dozen or more, coveting the chocolate donuts, saying they were for the people on the streets, which is how they met in the first place.

One rainy day before Moxie began working at the donut shop, she sat on the curb wondering where to go to get out of the rain and what to do when Miss Eunice passed by. "Here ya go, Sweetie Pie," she said, "put a little something in your stomach," handing her a donut. One thing led to another and before she knew it, Miss Eunice offered to let Moxie stay in her guest house in the studio apartment on her ranch land until she got established. Why would someone who she just met on the street be so generous? Moxie wondered. There was no way she'd offer her place, if she had one, to someone sitting on the curb looking all down and out. Her hair was knotted and greasy and it hadn't been combed in three days. Her face and clothes were filthy. The woman, for whatever reason, seemed to take an interest in Moxie.

"You get off your shift in twenty minutes, don't you? When the shop closes." Miss Eunice stated.

Moxie looked up at the round plastic clock that said, "Time to Get the Donuts" scrolled across the face. She wanted to bash it with her fist every time she saw it the way it aggravated and nagged at her every morning.

"Yes, twenty minutes left of my shift."

"I'll wait for you then, and give you a ride home."

Score! Moxie thought. Walking back and forth to work had grown old, very old, after a few months of doing it.

"Hop in." Miss Eunice said as leaned over from the driver's side and unlocked and opened the passenger side door. "In the back today, Toby," the old lady said pointing to the back seat. "Our friend gets the front seat today, buddy."

Moxie looked around but didn't see another body. She sat down and closed the passenger's side door.

"Toby, stop it!" Miss Eunice said, "Keep your nose to yourself. You can't have my bag of donuts. Just forget it and don't get any big ideas. You know they're for the street people."

Moxie looked quickly to the back seat, and again didn't see a soul but she did see the bag of donuts Eunice had put there.

"Alright, Toby. I'm sorry to be so cross with you. You be a good boy and I'll save you one chocolate donut. Just one, for dessert tonight. You know Mommy loves you."

Moxie, looked again at the backseat, this time turning around more fully thinking perhaps "Toby," whoever he was, was sitting directly behind her. As they drove on she was trying to decide whether to broach Miss Eunice and ask her whether the man had been around lately to check the "electrics." She didn't want to be accusatory, but, she thought sure she had locked her door to the studio apartment the day the charm bracelet went missing.

Moxie chewed on her lip not quite sure how to start the conversation.

"Miss Eunice, each month I've been living in the studio apartment you've said you had to let a man in to check the 'electrics' while I was at work. Has he come this month yet?"

"Next Wednesday he'll be in the area, so I'll let him in with my key when you are at work, if that's okay.

Moxie hadn't noticed any problems with the "electrics" and she wondered if there was a need to have an electrician come, but who was she to question.

"No need, I'll leave the place unlocked. There's like... nothing anyone would want in there anyway."

"Well, that will make things easy, dear. Thanks."

Miss Eunice drove on home and stopped in front of her guest house to let Moxie out.

"Thanks so much, Miss Eunice, I appreciate the lift." The young woman began to collect her backpack and readied to open the passenger side door.

Miss Eunice looked over her right shoulder in the direction of Moxie, then toward the back seat. "Oh, Sweetie Pie, that face of yours is one only a mother can love. Toby, don't you even think about jumping out of this car. If you get out, I'm warning you now, no chocolate martinis this afternoon. And forget the chocolate ice cream before bedtime."

Moxie looked once again into the back seat of the vehicle through the window as she was getting out of the car. As far as she could see, there was nothing but the bag of leftover chocolate donuts purchased at half price.

Chapter 7

With her tips, Moxie had just enough money to pay the cellphone bill. She stopped by the local phone store and paid the bill before heading home from work. She wondered how she was going to eat for the rest of the week. Her bread was almost gone and the peanut butter and jelly jars were nearly empty and ready to be scrapped.

Just as she came out of the phone store, Miss Eunice was passing by in her "beater car." She pulled over to the curb, rolled down her window, and asked Moxie where she was headed.

"Back to the apartment."

"Hop in!" The girl opened the door and got in.

"How are you doin' hon?" the old lady inquired.

"Getting by." *Like… barely*, Moxie thought.

"Why don't you come by later for dinner. Toby and I would love the company."

Moxie didn't particularly feel like hanging out all evening with Miss Eunice, but it's not like she had something better to do. Besides, she'd never been inside the woman's house before and was dying to see what it was like. Anything her landlady had planned for dinner beat what was on her menu. God, how she'd love to have some fruit or cheese or some fresh veggies.

"Thanks Miss Eunice, I'd like that. What time do you want me to come over?"

"Well, Toby likes his martini around 3:00. I've tried to tell him that's much too early for happy hour, but if he doesn't get his way, he gets snippy."

"See you in a few hours then, and thanks again for the ride. I do appreciate it."

As Moxie got out of the car Miss Eunice thought about how polite her tenant was. Upon first impression she looked like a punk teen with her purple hair, black fingernail polish, large tattoos on her neck and wrist, a nose ring and a pierced lip. The old lady knew she ought to be non-judgmental, so she was willing to give the girl a chance. After all, not everyone understood first impressions do matter to some people. Ah well, at least Moxie did have some social graces which was more than she could say for some young people. At least someone along the way had taught her a few of the basics. If only she'd get rid of the purple hair and nose ring and pierced lip, she'd face less opposition when trying to get a job. Good thing the donut shop was so hard-up for help. Otherwise, who would've hired the poor dear to represent their company.

"Oh, my," said Eunice as realized what else she was thinking. She turned to her friend in the back seat, "Toby, I told you not to let me be so close minded. Don't let me think like an old biddy!"

Chapter 8

Moxie decided she'd take a quick nap before heading over to her neighbor's for dinner. She unfolded the futon and spread her worn quilt over it. The coverlet was one of the few personal items she had carried from foster home to foster home over the course of her lifetime. The sterling silver foster mother had made it for her on her seventh birthday. In the center of the quilt was a large heart embroidered with the words *"With each passing day of you in my life, my heart grows fonder."* When the quilt was given to her, she never felt so loved and overwhelmed with happiness because it was a gift made especially for her. Over the years, in her darkest hours, Moxie often wrapped herself in the vivid colored quilt which helped to cheer her up and made her feel pretty. The spectrum of colors reminded her of her treasured carton of 64-color Crayola® crayons. The vibrant crayons looked like bright sherbet, good enough to eat. When she was a young child and even into her teens, she'd spent many hours coloring as a great escape from her sadness.

However, that foster home became just like all the others—only temporary. She ran her hands along the quilt wondering what the true story was. There were always vague excuses which came with every "transition" in and out of each foster home. It was the worst day when Moxie had to leave that couple. For as long as she lived, she'd remember her foster mother's final words. *"Listen to me child, we all have crosses to bear. Anything can be. Never, ever lose hope."*

Moxie laid down on the futon. It felt as oddly lopsided as her life so she pushed her hands into the fold trying to flatten it better. Digging her fingers further into the crease she felt something. With some effort she pulled out the item, along with a ten and five dollar bill and some singles. Her spirits soared. She had found her "big ticket item" along with some money she didn't remember even loosing. But, why hadn't she noticed the jewelry all the other times she looked for it?

Moxie immediately dialed the number she had gotten on Craig's List in the Lost and Found section, and the same man she had spoken with previously answered the phone. Again he sounded gruff and impatient.

"Hello, we spoke a few days ago when I called about a charm bracelet I found. You said your mother would call me back, and I haven't heard a word."

"Figures! My mother is getting funny. She can remember things from decades ago but not what I told her a day ago. I'll remind her again to call you."

The man took her name and cell phone number once again.

"Can I have your mother's number so I can call her directly?" Moxie wasn't going to let this second chance to collect reward money get away this time. She felt more in control of the situation once she had the lady's phone number and was no longer in a powerless position waiting for the woman to call back. Oh, how she hoped the bracelet was the one the woman had lost. She made a mental note to herself to call the lady first thing in the morning; she needed to get over to Miss Eunice's for dinner.

Chapter 9

"Now, what would you like to drink?" Miss Eunice asked as she let Moxie in the front door foyer which led into the living room. "Milk, ginger ale, sparkling cider, hot tea? I don't have too many choices since Toby and I don't usually entertain too much."

"Toby, I hear you. I know its past three o'clock. Let me get our guest situated first and I'll be in with your chocolate martini," the host said loudly as she looked in the direction of the hall off the living room.

"I'll have some cider." Moxie wondered why Miss Eunice hadn't offered her anything alcoholic, like the famed chocolate martinis Toby drank.

There was nothing Moxie would have liked more than a few glasses of wine or a few cans of beer, but Miss Eunice probably knew a drinking problem immediately. Except for this crazy thing of talking to the invisible "Toby" she seemed pretty with it for as old as she looked. Moxie didn't dare chance drinking anything stronger than cider. She'd managed to stay on the wagon and she didn't want to slip off. But, she sure would have relished the taste of an ice cold beer. She loved the way the bubbles danced effervescently across her tongue and tingled her throat when she swallowed. Once she got going.... well, she'd better not push her limits. Before she outgrew the system when she was at her most recent temporary living place, she had gotten pretty wasted by emptying some of the clear rum and gin out of the foster parents' liquor bottles replacing it with water when they were out of the house. It wasn't the first time she'd used that as a way of sneaking alcohol into drinks to get "shit-faced." Oh how her favorite foster mother would have cringed and scolded her if she'd heard her using that expression. Moxie remembered how the woman clucked her tongue every time anyone swore in her presence.

The girl had paid very dearly for her under-age drinking. The number of the times she tried to hide her throwing up, staggering and mumbled speech from her guardians was ridiculous. Foster parents were sick of having a constant barrage of visits from the social worker and the school counselor. It was why several of them ditched her. Now an adult, Moxie no longer needed friends to buy liquor for her but she didn't have an extra cent in her pocket so, she was living life sober—a different experience altogether.

Moxie scoped out the place while she waited for the host to return from the kitchen. Interesting, this place, she thought. Rustic ranch style on the outside, a veritable treasure trove on the inside. Trying to move around was next to impossible. Antiquities of all sorts, and kitschy collections from a multitude of eras, were stacked nearly to the ceiling and on top of all of the antique pieces of furniture. There was such an accumulation it was difficult to see what all was there. At first glance, Moxie saw boxes of old vinyl records, a large item resembling an arcade game which said "Wurlitzer" on it, books bound in linen, vintage toys and signs, sheet music and stained glass windows nearly large enough for a cathedral. There was even an assortment of what her foster mom referred to as "Sunday go-to-meetin' hats" and charming collector teddy bears. It was as if the woman's home was a museum of all things old and dusty.

The western style ranch architecture included an open floor plan with twenty-foot-high ceilings. Tall enough to house oversized, castle-proportioned furniture. A painted wooden horse which looked as if it belonged on a carousel caught Moxie's eye. Several side tables and curios cabinets held costume jewelry. Beautiful quilts softly draped the arms of the couches and laid across backs of easy chairs in complimentary colors. Some appeared to be sewn with vintage fabrics while others were made of newer material.

It looked as if someone had been trying to make some semblance of order out of it all. Many of the items were marked with price tags. Had the landlord just bought out someone's inventory or was she in the process of selling the items? It was difficult to tell.

What in the world was the old woman doing? Trying to see how many possessions she could amass in a lifetime? Moxie had never seen so much "stuff" in her life. *How do you live surrounded by so much crap?* Moxie thought. She reflected once again on how all her worldly possessions fit into one large duffel bag.

Nothing about the lady's personality indicated she might have a serious problem, other than her strange conversations with her invisible friend Toby. Perhaps the "beater car" should have tipped Moxie off the old lady liked old things. And the fact that ever since the first time they encountered each other she looked somewhat like a bag lady. Perhaps the woman didn't want to stick out like a sore thumb in designer fashions handing out donuts to the needy so maybe she opted for a shabby-chic persona.

The lady's guest apartment where Moxie lived was uncluttered except for a few cobwebs and more than acceptable. Moxie figured the reason the small place had old furnishings was because it was always tenant occupied. No need putting new furniture in a place where it would only get beat up.

Moxie's thoughts about the old woman's home were interrupted when she returned to the living room handing Moxie a tall glass of cider, "Here you go, Sweetie Pie, sit down and make yourself comfortable while I tend to Toby."

The young woman looked around the room wondering where her host expected her to sit. Moxie chose one of the newer chairs, and moved the clutter to the floor.

"Toby, honey, I'm coming with your chocolate martini. I'll be there in a minute. Let me fix one for myself too."

Miss Eunice went back into the kitchen, made the chocolate martinis and returned again setting one glass down in the living area on one of the low cocktail tables. She proceeded down the hall with the other glass in hand.

I wonder what those drinks taste like? Moxie thought, as she eyed the chocolate martini. *Maybe when my reward money comes in, I'll make a trip to the liquor store to get the makings to see what I am missing.* Although, she had eaten so many chocolate donuts over the past months, the thought of chocolate anything was not appealing. Not in the least.

Moxie's curiosity got the best of her, and when Eunice returned to the kitchen, she rose from her seated position. She continued to look around at the things that decorated the place, picking up some knick-knacks and examining them closely. Moxie knew nothing about antiques, but some looked very pricey.

Just as Miss Eunice returned to the living room, Moxie's phone rang.

"Hi," this is the lady calling back about the lost bracelet.

Moxie was taken by surprise. She never expected the lady to call back, and not now! It was an inconvenient time. "Yes, hold on a minute," she said, as she waded through the pile of boxes and furniture to the far corner of the enormous living room. She turned her back away from Miss Eunice, and stood behind a large armoire-type piece of furniture trying to get a little privacy.

"Is there somewhere we can meet so I can see if the bracelet you found is really mine? And you must understand upfront the reward comes with conditions." stated the lady.

Moxie was feeling a little anxious. She wasn't sure if it was because she felt like she couldn't breathe because she was so surrounded by so much stuff or whether she just was being paranoid. What if the lady said the bracelet was hers and made off with it when it really wasn't? Then, her "big ticket item" would be lost forever she'd be unable to collect anything from the pawn shop or a reward.

"Yes, I can meet you somewhere," said Moxie quietly, "do you live in town?"

"Never mind," said the lady. "How about we meet at Broadway and 9th at 8 a.m. on Thursday? There's a little park there. I'll be sitting on the bench, and I'll be wearing a gray felt hat with a flower on the side of it."

Eight a.m.? Moxie thought about her day off and having to make the trek into town so early. She could barely stand the thought. But the woman said the reward came with conditions, perhaps an early meeting was one of them. "Okay, see you then." Moxie hung up.

As she walked across the room in the direction of Miss Eunice her landlady yelled, "Toby! You have got to stop doing that! Every time I leave my drink on the table, and turn my back you knock it over and then it's gone. I'll have to fix myself another. No chocolate ice cream for you tonight before bedtime."

Moxie looked down at the dry, clean hardwood flooring under the table near Miss Eunice. She chuckled to herself thinking the woman was a little loony, but what a kind-hearted old lady.

Chapter 10

AT 6:30 A.M. ON THURSDAY, Moxie's alarm on her cellphone went off. She looked out the window and it was still dark. The last thing she felt like doing was getting out of bed at that hour and trudging back into town on her day off to meet the lady who might own the bracelet. It looked so cold out. Autumn was setting in deeper. The barren trees made her feel as if her surroundings in the foothills of the Sangre de Cristo mountain range look even more like a remote ugly wasteland. Each morning the temperatures dipped a little lower but there had yet to be snow. She reminded herself she'd better start looking for a few extra winter blankets for the futon, if she had any spare money to buy them.

If it wasn't for the promised reward money, Moxie would have canceled meeting the woman. Her stomach growled as she dressed and got ready to trek into town. She took the charm bracelet and put it in her front pants pocket where it seemed like a safer place than in her coat pocket. Grabbing her cellphone, out the door she went.

When she arrived in town, she looked at the time on her phone and realized she had a half an hour to spare. She decided to stop by the donut shop to say hey to Matt.

"Good morning, Moxie. What are you doing here this morning? You aren't on the schedule."

"Yeah, I know. I'm supposed to meet someone at the park on Broadway and 9th and I've got a few minutes to kill. Brrr, it's cold out." She wished she'd had a woolen scarf to wrap around her neck.

"That's why we're going through the coffee so quickly this morning. I'm about to pour out the remainder of the pot and brew up fresh. Here, finish what's left. It's on the house." Matt grabbed a white mug, emptied the pot and put the cup in front of Moxie. "Have the last coconut donut, too, finish it up."

Well, thought Moxie, *at least it is not chocolate and at least I'll have eaten something today. It may be all I'll get, so I'd better be grateful.*

"So, you're headed to the park on Broadway and 9th?" Matthew asked. "Be careful. It's pretty seedy in that part of Hopewell. I wouldn't talk to any strangers if I were you."

Great, she thought. *I've met someone on Craigslist and it's probably an ax murderer dressed up like an old lady luring people by offering a reward for a bracelet.* But what other choice did she have? Seventy-five dollars at the pawn shop. There was something about the lady's voice on the phone that made her curious about the "conditions" for the reward money. How could she tell what her top paying option was—the pawn shop offer or the reward money, if she didn't go talk to the lady who owned the bracelet?

Chapter 11

MOXIE WALKED THROUGH THE PARK. It was larger than some of the others in Hopewell, and with each step it confirmed what she already knew about many of the public grounds in the not so nice areas of town. Beer and liquor bottles, cigarette butts, empty syringes, fast food bags and wrappers were strewn all over the place. The roots of Moxie's hair tingled as she thought back to the worst three days of her life when she was completely homeless and had to sleep on a park bench. It was even more frightening than some of her worst nights when she heard Jared's father raging after a late night at the bar. At least then she'd had the security of a locked door between herself and the lunatic.

Well, hopefully her nights of sleeping outside in public places were over for a while. Miss Eunice had at least given her a place to live, if only temporarily. She looked around and didn't know what was worse —the garbage on the ground or the graffiti. Why did she expect to see just one bench with an old lady sitting on it? She was happy Matt had warned her about the area so she knew to be cautious.

Finally, after walking the grounds she noticed a wrought iron settee on the perimeter where a woman sat. She wore a gray felt hat with a flower on the side of it. Moxie wondered if it was Mildred, the lady she was looking for. The woman and her hat looked like something from another era, but she looked nice enough from a distance. Her head was bowed; she seemed to be in deep thought. Not a muscle was moving; her hands neatly folded together on her lap.

While she waited on the park bench, the woman reminisced about her cherished, lost bracelet. Many of the charms on it were gifts from her dear friend Eunice. When they met fifteen years ago, Mildred had encouraged Eunice to join her mental health support group. Eunice's husband had left her, and Child Protective Services was fighting to take away the foster child Eunice had come to adore. CPS said, "They needed to find a more stable two parent environment for the little girl." So, in order to help her friend, Mildred moved temporarily into Eunice's home and had also grown extremely fond of the child. But, it became apparent CPS wouldn't budge on their decision, and didn't consider "partnership parenting" between two friends an acceptable situation. Eunice and Mildred decided they wanted the best for the youngster so they didn't go to court to fight to keep the young girl. In her short life, the child had already been through enough.

It pained Mildred to see Eunice's deep hurts continue over having to give up her beloved foster child. Ever since then her dear friend struggled off and on with a bit of an addiction problem. Mildred tried to be sympathetic toward Eunice's tendency to hold tightly to and amass material possessions. After all the woman had suffered the loss of the two things that meant the most to her in life—her husband and foster child whom she hoped to adopt.

A few years after the removal of the foster child from Eunice's home, the two women had a heart-to-heart talk which helped Mildred better understand the woman's obsession with sweets and chocolate.

"How can you eat so many sweets in one sitting?" Mildred asked Eunice.

"I get such cravings."

"Have you ever tried to track when the yearnings come?"

"Oh, I know exactly when. I understand it, but I don't have willpower to do anything about it."

"Explain it to me then, will you?" said Mildred.

"I fret so about the little girl who was taken from my care. You know how dearly I loved her. I get real anxious not knowing how she is faring. My worry comes frequently and that's when I want to eat every sweet in sight. And chocolate really makes me feel better. Well... at least temporarily."

"Eunice, I understand where you are coming from, I really do. Frequently I think about her too, but at this point in her life there is nothing either you or I have any control over. Sadly, we've lost all contact with her. I pray she was placed in a good situation and I never give up hope of seeing her again.

"Maybe someday you can help me think like that," said Eunice.

"Only you can control how you are thinking," Mildred said with a gentle tone in her voice.

"Okay! Starting tomorrow, no more sweets or chocolate! When I start worrying about the little one, I'll think of something pleasant."

"Good idea! Think about the wonderful reunion we'll have when we see her, whether it's here on earth or in heaven. Plan our reunion party! How's that?"

"Can we put chocolate on the menu?"

Mildred couldn't help herself, she burst out laughing. "It's up to you my friend, it's up to you. You'll be the hostess of the party, so plan it however you'd like!" Mildred always loved her friend's sense of humor. A real bright spot in her life.

Over the years Mildred and Eunice had cried many tears and found faith together. They'd come far in their own personal growth by supporting each other's ambitions. Each had overcome difficult life challenges and struggles understanding success and personal fulfillment comes from one's own actions. The two women made a pact with each other to continue to attend the support group and to help young women who needed a hand-up, just as they did in their younger lives.

When the two women met, some people considered support groups a bizarre concept. Mildred had joined the group when her world was shattered and she was at the end of her rope for a variety of reasons. The support group was where Mildred met a person who saved her from self-destruction and inspired her to seek a new kind of life. She was intent on giving back.

Mildred was so caught up in her thoughts she didn't see Moxie approaching the park bench and wasn't aware of her presence.

"Excuse me, I'm sorry to interrupt your thoughts. Are you the woman who placed the ad in the Lost and Found on Craigslist?" Moxie asked, obviously startling the woman. The elderly woman gazed up looking as if she was trying to focus on the person in front of her. After a minute or two, she answered.

"No, but my son posted it for me," the lady said.

"Well, I'm Moxie. I hope I have the jewelry you are looking for."

"I hope so too. It's my treasured piece and it's been my saving grace. I've felt like I've been kind of lost without it. It keeps the memories of where I've been alive at the forefront of my mind. Did you bring it with you?"

The lady looked like any other ordinary woman in her late 70s or early 80s, not a particularly striking face but kindly, a grandmotherly type. Underneath the hat her hair appeared to be done up nicely. She wore an understated coat of makeup and her strawberry red lipstick was freshly applied. Her clothes looked like some kind of style gone by decades ago. Her floral dress was form-fitted at the bodice, accessorized by a slim fabric-covered belt, flaring to a calf-length full skirt. The woman wore white, wrist-length gloves, which if Moxie's memory served her right, were called "kid-skin gloves." When she was a little girl her guardian used to wear them when she arranged her freshly polished silver in the curio cabinet.

Moxie's eye was caught by a gleaming when the sun hit the diamond earrings that decorated the old lady's lobes. *Not a safe place to wear that kind of jewelry,* the young woman thought. If the woman didn't watch herself she was going to be out another piece of jewelry because it would be so easy to bump her off.

"Yes, I have the bracelet."

"Oh, good," said the lady, looking the young woman up and down, taking in her purple hair, the black lipstick, eyeliner and nail polish. One couldn't help but notice the tattoos and piercings.

"I need to introduce myself properly. I'm Mildred; pleased to meet you." She extended her white gloved hand and shook the young woman's.

What a god awful name. It's terrible, the young woman thought. It reminded her of the word mildew. Which is where the old lady's clothing looked like it came from—out of a storage box in some dank, dark basement somewhere. The gray felt hat with the flower on the side looked like something she had seen on a show about the Vaudeville era on MeTV. Well, it was memorable entertainment all right.

I shouldn't poke fun, Moxie thought, *my name certainly isn't much better.* It was beyond her comprehension why her birth mother hadn't named her something more common like Jennifer or Jessica. Perhaps then she would have fit in better with her peers.

She sat down on the park bench next to the old lady. Not wanting to seem overly anxious to get the reward money and run, she let the old woman initiate the conversation.

"So, tell me, where did you find the jewelry?

"On the railroad track between Kellenville and Hopewell."

"Really?"

"Yes, I walk the tracks like… every day on my way to work."

"Well, it's so far from where I think it was taken."

Moxie pulled the bracelet out of her pants pocket and showed it to the lady. "Yep, that's it!" said Mildred, smiling.

Great, thought Moxie, *now for my reward.* She began to hand over the bracelet, and then drew it back again.

"As I mentioned on the phone, there are conditions for the reward."

"Like what?"

"We'll get to that soon enough. You hold onto my bracelet and meet me right here on Saturday, at 2:00 p.m. Can you do that?"

"I suppose I could. I get off work on Saturday at like… 1:30 p.m. I could be over here to the park by like… two."

"Great," Mildred said, standing. "I'll see you then. And oh, one more thing. I promise you if you meet every condition, the reward will be much greater than you will ever expect."

Yeah, right, thought Moxie. But what did she have to lose? She was still in possession of the charm bracelet and at any time, she could still sell it off at the pawn shop for seventy-five dollars. She wondered why the woman trusted her to keep the bracelet.

Chapter 12

SHE HOPED THE WOMAN was going to show soon. Her rear end was freezing sitting on the metal park bench and her body heat was doing nothing to warm it. In fact, Moxie was growing colder by the minute. She checked her cellphone and it was ten minutes after two. Just as she considered leaving, Mildred came up from behind frightening her out of her wits.

"Sorry I'm running a little late. I had coffee with a friend of mine, and lost track of time. We got so involved in our conversation."

Both sat quietly.

"So," Moxie said, starting a conversation, "from the looks of the charms on your bracelet you've done some interesting things in your life. After all, people usually collect charms to remember landmarks or like...hobbies or trips or like... fun places, stuff like that. Charms are usually tokens of things that mean something important to somebody."

Mildred looked at the tattoo on the young woman's neck wondering about the significance of the date, thinking these days kid's versions of charm bracelets were tattoos. And as she looked at the young lady's bare cleavage, which seemed like a flashing neon light in a red-light district, Mildred pondered how the young woman could sit out in the cold with a flimsy deep vee-neck shirt and jacket which couldn't even be buttoned up there were so many missing. Brrrrrr, the old lady thought.

"The charms mean something to me alright; they are my lifeline. Like I told you the other day, I feel kind of lost without them."

Here then, you take it, and just like... give me the reward money. Moxie thought, but didn't say it.

"Did you bring the bracelet?" the old lady inquired.

"I did."

Moxie held the jewelry in the open palm of her hand. The elderly lady reached over and touched a few of the charms as if she was looking for one in particular. She turned the bracelet until she came upon the lighthouse. "This," she said, "is where it all started."

"That's nice," said the young woman completely uninterested.

"Can you meet me again? Same time, same place, the day after tomorrow?"

"I guess so." *You have got to be kidding,* Moxie thought. She felt really agitated wondering how long she had to play this game before she could get the reward money. Perhaps mugging the old coot for her diamond earrings would be easier and quicker than this lame idea of meeting conditions. What were the conditions she was trying to meet anyway? She didn't have a clue. She looked closer at the lady and noticed her earlobes were without jewelry that morning.

"Good, I'll see you then." The old lady stood, straightened the large diamond encrusted broach on the lapel of her jacket which complimented her floral, calf-length dress and walked off.

Chapter 13

Mildred looked the young woman up and down as she neared the park bench thinking she looked like she could use a good meal or two. Her head was down, her face looked ashen and she walked with lackluster steps.

"Hello, Moxie, fancy meeting you here!" She truly was glad to see the young woman hadn't jumped ship and came as promised. After all, she still had possession of her bracelet. At any time, she could take it to a pawn shop or sell it on the street. But, something was telling Mildred the girl needed more from her than the reward. But first, she wanted to get a better read on this young woman who was very obviously struggling. If she played her cards right, and if she was a good judge of character, perhaps this could develop into a pleasurable relationship.

"I haven't had lunch yet. Have you, Moxie?"

"No." There were many days she tried to stretch her nearly nothing budget.

"There's a little soup and sandwich shop, a block

over called Open Doors. How about we walk over and I'll treat you to lunch. Anything you want on the menu."

It sounded good to Moxie. She was so sick of eating the same old thing day after day – peanut butter and jelly sandwiches on stale bread and leftover donuts. She reminded herself to switch to boxes of mac and cheese for a while when the bread ran out. After all, that was something she might be able to get at the Dollar Store. Thankfully, every once in a while Miss Eunice dropped over with a leftover casserole or some kind of food she said she had too much of, otherwise she would have wasted away to nothing. All the walking back and forth to work was draining. Thankfully, Miss Eunice saved her from hoofing it several days a week saying she was going into town to get Toby his donuts.

"What will it be ladies?" the waitress asked.

"I'll have the B.L.T. and a cup of coffee." said Mildred. "Speak up dear, anything you want you can have. Make sure you don't leave the place hungry."

"I'll have the hot roast beef sandwich and a vanilla milkshake," said the young woman. Her mouth began to water, and she reflected hearty meals didn't come very often. The few times she went out to a meal with her friends, when she had friends, it was as if she was eating at places that only sold bird food —nuts, whole grains, seeds and some tofu crap. She always left the place feeling as hungry as when she arrived and it was not the kind of stuff she grew up eating in any of her foster homes.

"That comes with either fries or mashed potatoes, and the vegetable of the day is green beans," said the waitress.

"I'll take the mashed potatoes."

"Would you like gravy on them?"

"Yes, please," replied Moxie.

The server left the table and went to place the order.

"Thanks, Mildred. I could use a meal like this and they even have real mashed potatoes!" They sat quietly, not saying a word for a few minutes.

"So, did you bring the charm bracelet with you, again?" Mildred asked, hoping the young woman had. Without the jewelry around her wrist, she felt naked.

"So, tell me more about the charms on the bracelet. You said the lighthouse brought you out of the dark. What did you mean?"

"Well, I wasn't too much older than you, and my life was going in a wrong direction. Wait a minute, let me revise that. My life had never gone in the right direction right from the start until someone took pity on me and took me in. She was a life saver. She gave me this bracelet with my first charm. Sometime later, things began to brighten."

"It must have, when I look at these charms. They are not exactly costume jewelry," said Moxie, not meaning to say exactly what she was thinking aloud. She covered her mouth with her hand.

"Those charms have more value to me than you can ever imagine."

The waitress came to the table, and put down their food. Moxie inhaled the delicious aroma of the beef. She couldn't wait to dig in and was more interested in stuffing her mouth in that moment than stuffing her pockets with reward money. As they ate, they didn't say too much except to remark about the good food they were eating. Apparently the old lady frequented the Open Door a lot, and mentioned she had met many nice young women there. Evidently, it was a place particularly popular with the female set.

"Sure is nice to have someone to eat with," said Mildred. Moxie agreed silently. Even though she didn't want to admit it to herself, the times she'd been at her landlord Miss Eunice's for dinner she enjoyed more than just the nourishment.

As she ate, Mildred fingered every one of the charms skipping around the chain in no particular order, spending lots of time looking at some, and then shorter periods of time looking at others. It was as if she was partial to some charms more than others. "This one here was the second I received and it took me a long time to get it. But once I got it things began to change like quicksilver." The tiny wine goblet had what looked like a filament of metal running through it.

"Is that a token from a vineyard you like… visited once?"

"There was a vineyard alright."

Mildred placed the bracelet in the young woman's open hand and pressed it closed into a fist. She rose from her seat and went to the cashier and paid the bill while the young woman finished off every last bite of the highly-piled hot roast beef sandwich, the humongous mound of mashed potatoes, green beans and the tall vanilla milkshake. When she returned to the table the old woman looked at her silver watch on her wrist. Moxie noticed something tiny in a clear glass bubble dangling from it. If she wasn't mistaken, it looked like a mustard seed. Like the ones she'd seen in jars of pickles and potato salad. She wondered about the significance of carrying such an odd keepsake around on a wrist watch. She couldn't imagine what it symbolized. *Anyone can find out anything on the internet,* Moxie thought, *I think I'll Google it when I get home tonight.*

"Well," said Mildred, looking down at Moxie still sitting at the table, "let's shove off and plan to meet next week. Don't lose the bracelet—it means more than you will ever know."

"Next week? Look. This bracelet is obviously yours, there is no question. I see no need to keep dragging this out. I mean... you did promise a reward."

"Like I said, the bracelet comes with conditions. Meet me here on Tuesday at two o'clock. Will that work? Will you be in town for your job anyway?"

"Okay, see you at 2:00 then." *Maybe,* the young woman thought.

Chapter 14

MOXIE WOKE UP EARLIER THAN USUAL, but couldn't quite get a move on. She did everything she could to delay leaving for work. She thought about how the long walk to work was getting more difficult because the weather was getting colder each morning. She considered calling in sick but then thought about how empty her pockets were already since she had skipped work one day the previous week when she overslept and didn't show.

Just as she closed the door to her studio apartment to set off to work, Eunice was driving by. Her landlord pulled over and rolled down her car window. "Headed to work?"

"Yeah."

"Hop in! I'll give you a ride to town."

"Toby, in the back seat now buddy, there you go. Good boy," Eunice said in a sing-song voice. So, how are you today, dear?"

"Okay, I guess. It's just that I am tired of this game."

"What game?"

Then Moxie remembered Miss Eunice knew nothing of the charm bracelet and the promised reward money.

"Oh nothing. Just this walking back and forth to work. It gets like... old."

"What time do you get off work today?"

"Two o'clock and then I have to meet somebody." Only thing good about having to meet the other old lady again, was another free hearty lunch. All the items she'd seen on the menu last time they frequented The Open Door sounded heavenly.

"Look Moxie, I have some things that need doing around the house. Would you like to help me out a couple of afternoons a week when you get home from your job at the donut shop? I can't pay you in the traditional sense of the word, but I'll make it worth your while. I promise."

What was that supposed to mean can't pay you in the traditional sense of the word? She began recounting her memories of the day she met Miss Eunice. The old lady had been nothing but kind to her ever since. How could she say no? Guilt needled. If it hadn't been for the generosity of the woman she'd still be sleeping on a park bench.

The two women chatted back and forth until they arrived in front of the donut shop. Miss Eunice pulled over to the curb and the young woman turned to her landlord. "How about I start helping you tomorrow. I have the whole day off."

"Fine! Tonight I'll think about how you can help.

Toby and I will see you tomorrow. Can you get home alright?"

"Yes." Maybe one more trip down the railroad track and her timing would be just right and she wouldn't have to help Miss Eunice the next day after all.

Chapter 15

Mildred was already sitting at a booth when the young woman arrived at the Open Door Soup and Sandwich Shop for their two o'clock meeting. Moxie was beginning to get a little light-headed by the time she arrived. Unable to bear the thought of one more donut, she'd only had a cup of coffee.

Since the lunch rush hour was over, the two women placed their food orders immediately.

"I haven't got much time today. I've forgotten I have another commitment so I have to eat and run," the elderly lady said. The food came quickly, and once again, the young woman dug into the food with the hunger of a lumberjack.

The young woman watched the elderly woman as she picked at her Cobb salad. For the second time she felt as if their paths had crossed before, but she couldn't imagine where. It was kind of odd. Why was the woman dragging out the process of getting her charm bracelet back when she kept saying the bracelet was her lifeline?

Mildred watched the young woman eat as if she hadn't since their last meeting.

Moxie took the charm bracelet out of her pants pocket and set it on the table next to her plate hoping to start a conversation. Mildred reached across the table for the bracelet fingering each charm as if she was reacquainting herself once again with each one of them. The way she touched the charms it looked like she was using them as a rosary. She'd seen her foster mother, who often got slapped around, using her prayer beads every time things got overheated with her husband. She still remembered the words her foster mother repeated when she used the beads. *"Lord, help me find what I need in my life."* One time in a fit of rage the husband ripped the rosary out of her foster mother's hands and threw it against the wall.

"This one right here is one of my most meaningful charms," Mildred said examining the small silver baby bootie."

"Oh, do you have children?"

"That charm is all about baby steps, dear heart," said Mildred shifting in her seat.

Dear heart? Moxie thought, *save the niceties until you really know me.*

"I've got to run or I'll be late for my appointment. I'll take care of the tab on my way out. I saw you eyeing my pie. I'll have the waitress add the cost of another piece of pie to my tab, I'm sure you'd like a little dessert. Can we meet two days from now? I have someplace I'd like to take you. I need your help.

How about we meet at the donut shop when you get off work?"

"Ummm...I guess...." Moxie replied, shrugging her shoulders. She didn't know what was with old ladies thinking they needed her help.

"See you at 1:30 on Wednesday out in front of the donut shop."

The waitress rang up the check. Mildred paid and left. The server proceeded to the table and asked Moxie what kind of pie she'd like.

"Do you have lemon meringue today?"

"Sure do!"

"I'll have that." The last time she'd had lemon meringue pie was at the home of the nastiest foster mother of all of them. That woman did know how to make a good meringue pie. It was the best thing Moxie could think about her. How grateful she was she wasn't in that foster home for very long. She ate the pie quickly and put on her coat and left.

The days had gotten shorter, and by the time she reached her apartment it was a few hours before dusk and even colder.

Chapter 16

"CRAP!" MOXIE YELLED OUT AT 4:00 A.M. when she awoke and remembered she had left the charm bracelet on the restaurant table where she and Mildred were sitting the afternoon before. She jumped out of bed and began pacing. What was she going to do now? She knew she must get to the restaurant as soon as it opened to see if they found the bracelet.

She looked out the window and down the long driveway to the big house. What was Miss Eunice doing up at this hour? There were several lights on in her house and in the brightness of her porch light she noticed the beginnings of snow flurries. She looked at the clock on her cellphone and thought about the long trek into town. If she was going to reach the restaurant in time for their opening she'd probably have to leave in a half an hour. She was relieved to see when she Googled the restaurant, they didn't open until seven. She dreaded having to walk into town. During her recent conversation with Miss Eunice she said "Any time of day or night, if you need me, please call." Did a lost charm bracelet warrant calling the woman to ask her for a ride?

"Good Morning!" Miss Eunice said when she picked up the phone. Moxie had decided to wait until 5:30 a.m. to call her landlady even though her lights had been lit since 4:00 a.m. She hoped she wasn't asking for too much by requesting a ride.

"Moxie, you've been up since the wee hours, haven't you? Are you alright? I saw your light on in the apartment at 4:30 this morning. I was up then, too! We could've had a party. Good thing Toby was sound asleep at that hour, otherwise he would have insisted I get out the chocolate martinis and have a cocktail."

How could her landlady be so cheerful at this hour? All Moxie could think of was the lost bracelet and how careless she had been in leaving behind her ticket to the reward money—the jewelry.

"Well," Moxie said, hesitating for a minute, "I called to like… ask you a favor."

"What is it Sweetie Pie, what do you need?"

"I have a bit of an emergency this morning and need to get into town by about 6:30. Do you think you could give me a ride to town?" She didn't explain any further, and thankfully, Miss Eunice didn't probe.

"Certainly dear, you must be tired of walking to and fro from work. Give me twenty-five minutes, and I'll be dressed and ready to give you a ride."

"Oh, thank you. You don't know what this means to me."

"I think I do." Within twenty-five minutes her landlady had arrived and they had a quiet ride to town. Moxie looked out the window lost deep in thought. She was trying to decide what she'd tell Mildred if the waitress didn't turn in the bracelet to the manager and had made off with the piece of jewelry.

When her landlady dropped Moxie off at the donut shop, assuming she had to work, she was grateful she had taken her that far. There was still time to walk a few blocks over and be at the Open Door before the breakfast rush started.

Chapter 17

"Good morning, the doors are open!" the waitress said cheerfully when Moxie walked in the door. She inhaled the delicious smells of smoky bacon and eggs on the grill. It was good to be hit with something other than the smells of sickening sweet donuts coming out of the fryer first thing in the morning.

"I'm looking for the server who was here yesterday afternoon. Is she around?" Moxie inquired.

"Not in today. Can I seat you and take your order?"

"I'm not here for breakfast. I left something behind on the table yesterday afternoon before closing. I was hoping the waitress left it with a note or something."

"What was it? I'll look around for it," the waitress said nicely.

"A bracelet with like… charms on it."

"Have a seat." The waitress motioned to a stool at the counter, poured Moxie a cup of coffee and disappeared in the back. She hadn't asked for the cup of coffee and she hoped she could scrape together enough change to pay for it. She took a sip of the steaming hot coffee and glanced over in the direction of the table where she was sitting the afternoon before. The table was empty except for the usual salt and pepper shakers, a napkin dispenser and a few condiments. She saw nothing extra on the top of the table – like the bracelet she needed to find. What would she say to Mildred if she couldn't find it? She began wringing her hands as she listened to the waitress asking someone in the kitchen area whether they had seen the bracelet.

"I don't see it anywhere, and I pretty much turned the place upside down. No note or anything in the place where we usually put lost and found stuff." The waitress said as she came through the swinging door back from the kitchen into the front of the restaurant.

"I hate to be a pest, but, could you call the waitress who served me yesterday afternoon to see if she found it? It's like... important."

The server looked at her watch. "It's a little early. But, yeah, okay. Give me a minute. Let me take this customer's order first."

"No answer," the waitress said as she stood in front of Moxie making the call. "And her voice mail isn't picking up either. Tell you what, leave me your cellphone number and your name. When Chloe comes in, the waitress who was here yesterday, I'll ask her about your bracelet."

Moxie grabbed a napkin on the counter, jotted down her name and phone number and handed it to the waitress. The waitress proceeded to stuff the napkin into her pocket and watched as Moxie scrounged for change in her backpack. The server came closer to Moxie and whispered into her ear, "You know what, don't worry about it. It's only a cup of coffee. It's on me this morning."

"Thanks so much." said Moxie quietly, as she slipped out of the Open Door. She had done the same for a few people over at the donut shop.

Chapter 18

A VINTAGE PINK CADILLAC with what looked like fins running along the side pulled up in front of the donut shop at precisely 1:30 p.m. The driver leaned over and rolled down the passenger side window. "Yoo-hoo! Moxie! Hop in." It was Mildred's voice calling out.

Oh no, don't tell me I've got to ride around in that thing! What if one of my friends sees me! Moxie thought. She instantly felt like crying because she suddenly remembered the closest thing she had to homeys were the two old ladies, Miss Eunice and Miss Mildred. How pitiful was that for a twenty-three year old? Very!

She opened the car door and peered in at the white leather seat and dashboard. The steering wheel was so big it looked like the Hula Hoop she'd seen at the second hand shop. Moxie pushed aside an assortment of candy wrappers toward the middle of the bench seat and got in. Turkish Taffy, Mary Janes and Bit O'Honey wrappers were everywhere and several empty boxes of Jujubes littered the seat. What is it about old women and their sweets? It was kind of comical. And where was the old lady getting this old school candy, anyway? Who was her supplier?

The car looked like no other car Moxie had ever ridden in before. A pair of fuzzy dice dangled from the rear view mirror. Moxie wondered if the woman's house was just as tacky.

Why was she worrying about what she looked like riding around in the pink Cadillac, anyway? What was she going to tell Mildred about the bracelet? She couldn't stand the thought of admitting she had left it at the café. On second thought, why did it matter? Did the woman mean that much to her? Well, the reward money certainly did. She'd just have to say she didn't bring the bracelet with her if the lady asked. It was the only way to bide some time until she heard back from the waitress. And why hadn't the waitress called back anyway? The bracelet was probably long gone, either picked up by another customer at the diner or perhaps the waitress made off with it herself.

"Good afternoon, Mildred. Where are we off to?"

"I'm having a hard time making some decisions, I thought maybe you could help me. I need someone else's opinions on some fabric. I thought we'd take a little trip to the sewing shop over on the east side of town and then I'll drive you home."

"Sewing shop? Well, I don't know anything about

sewing and fabric but I'll go along. What are you sewing?"

"Haven't determined that yet, I have a few patterns I'm considering." Moxie looked over at Mildred and noticed her outfit. She hoped the old lady was going to sew herself some trendier clothes—Good Lord! Her gray wool-pleated skirt and white blouse with rounded collar were from some other era. As was her pale pink cardigan which hung off her shoulders with a sweater clasp. Talk about vintage! And her shoes and thin white socks cuffed at the ankles—well, she'd never seen anything quite like them anywhere. How far back into the cave did the old lady have to go to dig those things out?

"Have you been sewing for a long time, Mildred?"

"Long enough."

Moxie had hoped by making conversation with Mildred about sewing she wouldn't think to ask about the bracelet. So, she continued to ask her elderly friend more questions about her craft hobbies. Like she was really interested. Seriously, who cared about something as old-school as that?

Until then, the bracelet was the only thing they had talked about in their encounters, which Moxie had grown tired of and had decided perhaps it would be easier to take the bracelet to the pawn shop rather than going through any more "meet-ups." Well, those meetings had probably come to an end anyway seeing how she had lost what may have been her "big ticket item" out of her sorry life. Moxie felt the onset of despair. The dark cloud already hanging over her head seemed to be settling in even deeper. How could she have been so stupid to leave something so important to her future behind? At least she knew where she had stashed away one charm that had fallen off the bracelet the day she discovered it on the railroad track. But how much money could a little cross be worth? Ten or fifteen dollars? A lot of good that was going to do.

The young woman looked out the car window and saw what looked like sleet beginning to shower down. Even darker, drearier days would soon be arriving with the full onset of winter.

"Here we are!" said Mildred cheerfully as they approached their destination.

"I wish I'd brought a coat."

"Me, too!" the old lady said as she steered into the parking space, coming to a slow stop in front of the fabric shop. Opening the car doors, they both stepped out into the cold dampness. Moxie trailed behind the old lady into the store with her eyes downcast, hugging herself to keep warm. She could have cared less what the store had to offer. At least the trip came with benefits—a ride home.

As soon as they entered the shop, the clerk greeted Mildred by name. She began pacing up and down, aisle after aisle, looking at all the fabric. Moxie looked at a rack of buttons and trims and other sewing accessories. She had no idea there would be so much stuff in a sewing store.

"Moxie, dear, can you help me with these bolts of fabric." She walked over to where Mildred had pulled out a large selection of fabrics and had set them down on the large flat counter where the store attendants measured and cut fabric.

"I'll be there to help you in a few minutes," yelled out the clerk from the cash register. She appeared to be the only person working.

"No problem, we have lots of decisions to make, it will be a while till we are ready," said Mildred, turning to the young woman. "So dear, what colors do you like?"

"Oh, I don't know. I've never put much thought into sewing before." Moxie looked down at the chosen selection. Mildred picked a few bolts up and began to hold them up next to each other, mixing and matching, seemingly unsatisfied. Moxie began to paw over the bolts not really knowing what she was looking for or what she was supposed to be doing. She set a few materials aside she liked. She walked between the aisles and pulled out other bolts that caught her eye. Many complemented the ones she favored. She took them back to the large counter and compared the fabrics. Some, upon further inspection, didn't match or look good with each other. Others were spot on—a perfect complement. She continued to browse the store and soon she became totally absorbed with what she was doing. At first she was drawn to many of the darker colors and patterns but as time went on, she found she had eliminated them for lighter, brighter colors.

"Let me see what you've got over there, dear," Mildred said, walking over to the area of the large counter where Moxie had amassed a nice collection. Some were solid colors, others floral and even a few stripes and plaids were in the mix but the overall assortment was color cohesive.

"You've got quite an eye for color and pattern," said Mildred smiling broadly. I like what you've picked out.

"How much fabric do you need?"

"Let me see, I've got several patterns with instructions in my purse."

She watched Mildred as she walked over and picked up her large purse that looked like a carpetbag from the counter. Mildred peered inside the bag and then set it down. "I've forgotten my patterns," she said with a disappointed tone in her voice.

The clerk came over to the counter where they measured and cut yardage. "Are you ready for my help? Have you chosen some fabric?" The clerk looked down at the pile Moxie had in front of her. "Oh, my! What an interesting assortment you've selected. It's stunning and very creatively chosen. My goodness!" the clerk said, eyeing Moxie's purple hair, nose ring and pierced lip. "What are you making?"

"Oh, I don't know how to sew. It's for my friend here," Moxie said pointing to Mildred. Moxie kind of surprised herself. It was the first time she had referred to Mildred as her friend.

Mildred turned to the clerk. "I just realized I've forgotten my patterns and instructions. Is there a possibility you can set these fabrics aside? I'll be back tomorrow when I have them with me. Then I'll know how much yardage I need."

"I don't see why not, after all I am the manager," said the woman with an impish smile on her face. "What time do you think you can be here tomorrow?"

"I'll be here when you open. At 10:00 a.m."

"Great, it's usually quiet for the first half hour or so then—boom—the rush begins. Sometimes I feel like we shortchange our customers because unfortunately I am the only one here and can't give the attention our customers deserve."

The two women left the shop and the car ride to Moxie's apartment was pleasantly filled with more talk of fabric, color and other sewing matters.

Mildred parked in front of Moxie's door and turned to her. "I had a very pleasant afternoon. I learned something about you. I think you've missed your calling."

"What do you mean?"

"You have quite a talent for color. Your choices were spot on, as far as I am concerned. You need to do something with your good design sense. Let's work on that. Shall we?"

Moxie thought back to her school days. Art was her favorite subject. Her teachers had tried to encourage her but, without a parent to provide additional support and encouragement for her talents, she floundered, never finding any particular direction. Just trying to survive all the foster home transitions was hard enough, never mind trying to pursue her interests.

"When will I see you again?" asked the older lady.

"I'm not sure. I don't have my schedule from work for next week."

Mildred pulled a pencil and paper from her purse and proceeded to write down her phone number and gave it to the young woman. "Call me when you can, and bring along the bracelet next time we meet."

Suddenly, Moxie's face paled and her spirits sank. It had been an enjoyable afternoon even though the thought of the lost bracelet had put a damper on her high spirits. In fact, it had been the best day she had had in a long, long time.

Chapter 19

Screw it! Moxie thought, the moment she opened her eyes. She'd just have to be late for work. She had to return to the Open Door Soup & Sandwich Shop where she left the bracelet to see if she could catch the waitress who was there the day she left it behind. Her stomach growled with a vengeance. She hadn't had a thing to eat the day before other than a few donuts at the end of her work shift.

Despite the great afternoon she'd had with Mildred, she sank into a dark hole when she got home from the fabric shop. When she began thinking of the bracelet, and the fact that she hadn't gotten a phone call from the waitress at the Open Door, eating was the last thing on her mind. She spent hours searching Craigslist and other internet sites to see if anyone had posted the bracelet back in the Lost and Found section. Worse, it would be just her luck if the waitress had already sold it on the street. If that was the case, she'd kill the waitress. She put herself down for leaving the bracelet behind by calling herself every self-degrading swear word she ever knew.

Jumping out of bed, she threw on the first thing warm she found in her closet. She looked in the mirror at her hair, shivering. The day before she had decided once the purple dye had faded, she couldn't afford to re-color it. She needed every cent she had to put food in her stomach and to purchase a second blanket and boots for winter. She walked out the door and started down the railroad track pondering where the money would come from for the logs she'd need to fill the wood stove all winter.

"All God's angels come to us disguised," Moxie's favorite foster mother always claimed. Like an angel dressed like a lumberjack was going ride in on a John Deere with a trailer, bringing her wood and stack it up like packages tied up with string. *Yeah, right!* Moxie thought mockingly. *Seriously. Like it could happen. After all, she was in the Sangre de Cristo Mountains, whoo-hoo, where the elevation was high and temperatures got cold as the devil.* Moxie laughed at her own poor joke. It was the first time in a long time she had laughed at anything.

"Good morning, Moxie! Surprised to see you here at the Open Door." Moxie looked in the direction of the voice, and saw Mildred sitting in one of the booths.

Moxie froze! Oh God, how could she ask for the waitress who served them the day before without Mildred hearing? She felt doomed.

"Come on over, Moxie." She walked over to the

booth where Mildred was sitting. "Have a seat, and have some breakfast with me. It will be nice to have company this morning. I'll treat you." How could she refuse? Her stomach was growling big time.

"That's awful nice of you, Miss Mildred. First I have a phone call I need to make. I'll be right back." She went outside the restaurant and called the donut shop on her cell phone.

"Hi Matt, it's Moxie. I'm not going to be in today. I've had like... an emergency. Something just cropped up, otherwise I would've called you last night." She could tell by Matt's voice he was seething.

"Yes, I'll be in tomorrow as scheduled." She listened as he spoke of the challenges of being short-handed. He restated his hope very sternly she would be there as promised the next morning.

She hung up the phone, and thought for a few minutes about how she was going to handle the issue of the bracelet. If the waitress who served them the previous day was not there, she'd try to fill her breakfast conversation of sewing shop talk again. Once back inside she sat down across the table from Mildred.

"Is everything okay, dear?" Mildred asked, noticing the young girl looked as if she hadn't slept much. She looked more drained every time she saw her.

"Yes. I really enjoyed our visit to the sewing shop yesterday, Mildred."

"Did you dear? Why, I did too. I have my patterns and instructions with me this morning and I'll head over to pick up the fabric after breakfast. I loved the choices you picked out yesterday. Say, I saw a sign at the fabric shop. I am interested in finding out more of the details. They're offering a basic class on quilting. Would you be interested?"

"Oh, I really don't have extra money for things like that. Besides, I don't know how I'd like… get back and forth without a car." Although, if sewing and quilting was even half as much fun as picking out the fabrics for a project Moxie thought perhaps she'd like to learn something about it. *Forget it,* she thought, she really didn't have an extra cent to her name.

"Just out of curiosity, how much is the class and how often is it?"

"I'm not sure. Those are the kinds of details I want to find out about."

The two chatted back and forth amiably for a few minutes about sewing, when Moxie noticed something gleaming next to the napkin dispenser and salt and pepper shakers at the head of the table. She tried to look closer without being obvious, and saw it was the charm bracelet.

What now? Should she mention the bracelet or act as if she hadn't seen it? Just as she finished the thought, Mildred picked up the bracelet and began looking at each and every charm individually as she had each time she had it in her hands, again acting like was her rosary.

"Isn't it funny how things have a way of getting back to us, Moxie?"

"I guess so."

Mildred put the bracelet down and drummed her fingers on the table as if she was trying to figure out what to say next. She had a look on her face Moxie had never seen before—equal parts annoyance and disappointment.

Here it comes, thought Moxie, *she's going to ream me out*. She braced herself, waiting for a scolding.

Mildred picked up the bracelet again and resumed twirling it until she came to a charm which looked like a box. She looked it over. "I guess we won't open Pandora's Box. Let's just say when things are meant to come back to us, it happens." She handed the bracelet over to Moxie.

Moxie felt a ten ton brick of relief drop from her chest. *Is this lady forgiving me or what?* She wondered why Mildred hadn't pocketed the bracelet right then and there. After all, she owned it and she had mentioned several times it was her lifeline. One time she even referred to it as her "saving grace." The young woman didn't know what that meant but the bracelet did seem to have great sentimental value. She couldn't believe Mildred would trust her any longer with it.

"Well, dear, did you get enough breakfast this morning?"

Moxie reached down and rubbed her stomach. "I sure did. I'm stuffed. Miss Mildred, I, umm… we can't continue meeting this way. I mean… you keep buying me meals and I can't return the favor."

"Oh, dear, don't even think about it. Besides, I'm

enjoying your company," Mildred said patting the top of the young woman's hand. They said their good-byes and Moxie headed down the railroad track for "home."

Chapter 20

"I'm sorry, I'm going to have to let you go," Matt said the next morning.

"Let me go? What do you mean?"

"I can't depend upon you."

"Oh come on, just because I had an emergency yesterday? I've only missed work like… once."

"No Moxie, there have been too many other times you haven't shown or were late. I have a business to run here, and I need to find someone who is going to show up and take the responsibilities of the job seriously. Your last paycheck will be ready for you on Friday. Stop by and pick it up."

Moxie knew from Matt's tone, it was final. There'd be no use in trying to talk him into letting her stay.

She walked out the door, and began the walk back through town towards home when a car pulled up beside her on the sidewalk. At first she didn't hear the car. She had her earbuds on and was listening to loud music trying her best to drown out her sorrows. Then she realized the vehicle was "the beater."

"Hop in if you're headed home. That's where I am going." Moxie opened the door and got in. "Off work already this morning? Short shift?"

"Yeah." Moxie didn't qualify her answer. Last thing she wanted Miss Eunice to know was she had been fired.

"Can you help me this morning when we get back? You've really been of great assistance, and I appreciate it."

For the past few weeks, Moxie had been helping Miss Eunice clean out closets, rooms and drawers. They'd stacked stuff Eunice no longer wanted in her basement and were making good headway. The living room had become almost livable. Moxie couldn't imagine how one person could accumulate so much stuff and who would want some of the ancient things such as the Remington typewriter. *How could you use it to type anything?* The young woman wondered. *Where were the control, alt, delete keys anyway?* And then there was the hand-cranked adding machine and the cash register without a credit card scanner. Why in the world would anyone need extinct machinery? They were nothing but relics.

"Miss Eunice, can I ask you a question?"

"Sure dear."

"What are you going to like… do with all the stuff we're cleaning out?"

"I don't know dear. We'll see when the time comes whether someone else is worthy of having it. For the time being, this is something Toby and I have wanted to do for a long, long time. Straighten things out. I told Toby, if he stays out of the way today, I'll give him a donut this afternoon when we're finished. He'll complain. These are two day olds," Eunice said, picking up the brown bag of donuts spotted with grease. "I picked them up yesterday when the shop was about to close and forgot to take them around to the street people. I didn't see you yesterday at the donut shop. You must not have been working. Remind me dear, to give a donut to Toby when we are finished sorting through my stuff."

Moxie still had yet to see this Toby character Miss Eunice talked about.

Chapter 21

MOXIE STARED OUT THE WINDOW of her apartment wondering how could she feel so bummed because she was without a job at a lowly grease pit. Absorbed in thought, she saw something go by the window but it didn't register until it was almost out of sight. Was that the back end of Mildred's pink Cadillac she saw out of the corner of her eye? It had to be. Who else drove around in a car like that? She wondered what in the world Mildred was doing. She walked over and sat in front of her computer and stared at the screen aimlessly. Suddenly, there was a sharp rap at the door. She rose from her seat and opened it.

"Mildred, what are you doing here?"

"I hope I haven't disturbed you dear. I was going to call but, I didn't have your number. Only way I knew how to get in touch was to stop by. I'm glad I drove you home the other day, so I'd know where you live. I wanted to tell you more about the quilting class that starts next week, and see if you wanted me to enroll you."

"No, I'm sorry, I can't."

"Sure you can!" said the older woman.

"As much as I think I might like to, I really can't."

"Sure you can, there's always ways around things. You know what they say, 'There are no problems in life, only solutions.'"

Moxie remained quiet thinking about the adage and wondered why no one had ever pointed that out to her before.

Mildred looked at Moxie and wondered what her sudden withdrawal from the conversation was all about. Perhaps it was wrong to step in and maybe she should've minded her own business. But, she felt sure Moxie might be interested in the bargain the fabric shop manager had worked out with Mildred on the young woman's behalf.

"Moxie, Meredith is in dire need of help at the sewing shop. She was so impressed with your eye for color and pattern she said she'd like to hire you if you're willing to be trained as her assistant. She needs someone to give advice to customers on fabric purchases when they come in the shop and she needs help at the register. She can't pay you a lot but, in the bargain she'll throw in the basic quilting lesson as part of your training. I've signed up, too. Even old ladies like me like to learn new things. Don't worry, I'll see to it you get back and forth to work and to the quilting classes."

"Really?" Moxie asked with surprise in her voice. "You like… did that for me? You asked the manager if she'd hire me?" She couldn't believe someone who barely knew her would look out for her like that. And what timing! She'd been so anxious and hadn't been sleeping worrying about where she was going to look for employment.

"What are you doing now? Are you on your way into work?" asked Mildred, looking at the young woman's ratty bathrobe.

"Nothing." She hadn't even combed her hair or brushed her teeth, and it was already 10:00 o'clock. Where had the morning gone?

I'll wait here while you go take a shower and get cleaned up. Then I'll drive you over to the fabric shop and you can discuss the terms of your employment with Meredith.

"Would you?"

"Certainly!"

The young woman set off in the direction of the shower.

"Oh, Moxie, by the way, you might want to put on the nicest clothes you can find. After all, this is still an interview of sorts, and there might be customers in the store. You'll want to give a good first impression. And about the charm bracelet, wear it. It will look nice on your wrist." The elderly woman thought back to her first jobs, and remembered how difficult it was to pull together something decent to wear, fit for work.

Chapter 22

"Good luck, dear. Take as much time as you need. I'll be waiting right here in the car with my book. When you're finished working out your employment start date and schedule with Meredith, I think we ought to have a little celebration. How about we head over to my house. It's only a few blocks away and I'll fix us a little lunch."

About forty-five minutes later, the young woman opened the passenger side door of Mildred's car and hopped in. Mildred put down her spiral notebook and pen and put the keys in the ignition, starting the car.

"How did it go, dear?' Mildred asked before she began backing up the car. She'd never seen the young woman look so cheery.

"Great. I start on Monday. I'll work from like… 11:00 a.m. until like… 5:00 on Mondays, Wednesdays, Fridays and Saturdays. It's not going to be forty hours at the start but we might work up to it. Mrs. Wilson, ummm… Meredith, said, 'we'll see how it goes.'

And she said the quilting class is on Monday and Wednesday evenings from like… 6:00 to 8:00 p.m., and she said she'd pay the class fee and for my time to take the course because it's part of my training. She said to pack something to eat on Mondays and Wednesdays and take a break at like… between 5:00 and 6:00 p.m. to eat dinner before the quilting class. Mrs. Wilson…ummm…Meredith isn't teaching it. She's bringing someone else in who's like... an expert in sewing everything."

We've given the right person a chance, Mildred thought as she listened to the young woman ramble on excitedly. But she knew from her experience, one baby step at a time was the best approach. She was so hopeful the young woman could rise to her other expectations. She listened to Moxie describe more details of her employment and her responsibilities. Over the years Mildred learned you never knew what might ignite an interest in young women who were lost and floundering. Granted, she hadn't known Moxie very long, but still it warmed Mildred's heart to know she could be in part responsible for getting this girl off to what might be new beginnings.

Moxie felt as if she had just hit the jackpot. The way she figured it, she'd be getting close to thirty hours of work a week at the sewing shop. Although there'd be no tips like at the donut shop, she couldn't help but think this job would be more interesting and have a better chance for pay increases. She could hardly wait to get started.

"I promised you lunch. Let's head over to my

house. We're very close." A few minutes later, she pulled the pink Cadillac into her circular driveway. The young woman's eyes widened when she saw Mildred's house. It was even larger than Miss Eunice's and there was nothing tacky about it. Quite to the contrary. Classic elegance. It seemed out of place surrounded by the rugged Sangre de Christo Mountains.

As Moxie sat in the living room taking in her beautiful surroundings, Mildred fussed in the kitchen with lunch. She inhaled the sweet, yet slightly spicy fragrance of the roses sitting on the coffee table in front of her. She ran her hand over the beautiful fabric of the sofa, trying to think what the fabric was called. Brocade, perhaps? She'd ask Mildred. Moxie thought back to a similar sofa one of her foster mothers had years ago. She thought again how she wished that woman had adopted her. Surely her life would have been much different—problem free since that woman seemed to have anything she wanted or needed. Her mind drifted with the thought she'd better get more acquainted with various kinds of fabric if she was going to start working in a sewing shop.

Her thoughts of how everything in the old lady's house seemed to have its own place was interrupted by Mildred's voice.

"Moxie, dear, come on into the dining room, lunch is ready." Moxie rose and walked into the dining room. Everything in Mildred's house looked like the images she'd woven in her mind throughout her childhood of what a perfect life looked like. The table was beautifully set with china and silver candelabra on a crisply starched tablecloth. She immediately noticed goblets on the table wondering whether the elderly lady had really given her a glass of white wine with her lunch. If so, she was certain it was going to be a whole lot better than any of the gut rot stuff she used to drink.

"I love your quilted table runner, Mildred."

"Thank you dear, I love it too. A very precious friend made it and gave it to me as a gift and I haven't taken it off the table since. I even use it to top off a tablecloth.

"And those roses in the living room. What are they? They're so fragrant!"

"Oh, those are my damasks! Which are heirloom roses first cultivated back in the Biblical times introduced in Europe by the Crusaders. I have a large bush of them on the south side, tucked right up against the house. They are climbing everywhere. You ought to go outside and see them. I brought in the very last blooms of the season. Good thing I did. Tonight, according to the paper, we're going to get a hard frost which will probably kill them. They aren't particularly good for cutting and bringing indoors so they won't last long. But, oh, how I love the scent of them in the house. "

Both women sat down and reached for the napkins beside their plates.

"Linen?" Moxie asked, as she placed it in her lap.

"Yes, linen."

"Whatever we're having smells delicious, Mildred. Thanks for having me."

"Why really dear, it's nothing—just a little shrimp salad. I had a friend over yesterday and there was just enough left for you and me today." The young woman looked down at the large flaky croissant stuffed full with shrimp salad spilling out. And there were thin slices of red apples and a small bunch of green grapes on a bed of romaine lettuce. It all looked so inviting. Moxie reached for her wine goblet and took a sip. She was disappointed to find out the glass held ginger ale but she thought about how even something as simple as that looked so special in a fancy glass. Oftentimes water from the spigot was the best thing she could find to drink at her place. *Why would the old lady frequent the Open Doors Soup and Sandwich Shop if she could eat and exist like this at home?* the young woman thought feeling a little befuddled.

"Mildred, what's the fabric on your sofa called? Is that like… brocade?"

"Yes, dear, it is. Some people call it silk brocade but brocade will do. Why do you ask?"

"I'm just trying to remember the names of different kinds of fabric to like… educate myself for my new job."

"You'll learn quickly, dear, if you're truly interested. Don't worry. When you're around fabric daily, you'll be able to distinguish different kinds of materials in no time.

Moxie looked across the room at the sheer curtains at the windows. "What's the gauzy stuff?"

"Voile," said Mildred.

She sure knows her fabrics, Moxie reflected. The elderly woman must have spent a lot of time hanging around sewing shops. The young woman knew learning about the sewing accessories in the store would also be a part of her training. She had to admit she was rather excited about the prospect of learning stuff at her new place of employment.

"Mildred, I love the bright graphics on the tablecloths they use at the Open Door. They're so cheery. They remind me of sitting at a kitchen table in a sweet grandmother's cottage."

"Those dear heart, are vintage tablecloths made out of something called bark cloth. Some people call it rhino cloth because of the slightly textured look and feel. Those table linens were very popular for a few decades from 1940 to around the 1960s. Many people covered their cocktail tables and card tables with bark cloth or used the fabric on upholstered chairs and slipcovers or for curtains. It's my understanding a very generous lady, someone in the community, donated all those linens to the Open Door to help them get started in business. They're charming, aren't they?"

"Oh, yes, they add to the ambiance and coziness of the place. I love the cherries and strawberries and the bright florals on them."

When the fabric discussion ended, Moxie decided to bring up the charm bracelet. She took it off her wrist and laid it on the dining room table. As she had gotten to know the elderly woman, her curiosity had grown about some of the charms. How did they relate to the life the old women led? Some of the charms seemed strange. Like the silver charm that looked like a short piece of rope knotted at the end, the tiny church with the red door and the miniature hand mirror made to look like shattered glass. What might they signify in Mildred's lifetime? The young woman glanced at the cruise ship charm on the bracelet. Perhaps, she thought, the boat and the rope were related in some way. After all, ropes were needed to tie up ships at ports of call.

"Moxie, I've had you carrying the bracelet around with you. I'm a little concerned it may get lost. Why don't you keep it at home from now on, in your dresser or some other safe place."

Had the old woman forgotten about the reward money? Moxie wondered.

"Mildred, why don't I just like... give you the bracelet now." Moxie extended her hand with the bracelet in her fist, trying to hand it to Mildred. She had hoped her gesture would trigger Mildred's memory of the reward due her for finding the bracelet. After all, it was what was promised.

Mildred ignored the opened hand with the bracelet in it. "That's okay, dear, you take it and keep it safe. Someday soon, I'll want it back.

"But, you keep telling me it's like... your lifeline. Are you sure you wish for me to hang onto it?"

"Yes Moxie, I trust it in your hands for safekeeping," Mildred said confidently.

Now, wasn't that a new concept? Someone trusted

her. It made her want to keep the bracelet safe that much more.

When they were finished eating, Moxie rose from her seat at the table. "Sit, Mildred, I'll do the dishes. You cooked." She didn't want her elderly friend to think she was a freeloader. It was the least she could do for the lady who had been buying her meals and now had gotten her a job.

"How about we do the dishes together? Many hands make work light. It's been so nice to have you here with me this afternoon. I like not having to sit at this big table alone. I guess you're anxious to get home. You've got a big week coming up with your new job." The two cleaned up the lunch mess and were enjoying visiting so much they moved into the living room. Before they knew it, it was 4:30 and the two women headed for Moxie's apartment.

Mildred dropped the young woman off in front of the guest cottage. Moxie said her goodbyes and went inside. She watched out the window as the pink Cadillac drove off, proceeding up the long driveway towards Eunice's place. Moxie wondered what the old lady was doing. Was she going up to the wide spot in the road and turning around?

Moxie went over to her dresser, pulled open the top drawer, placing the charm bracelet in the wad of tissue holding the loose charm in the back right hand corner of her sock and underwear drawer.

One by one, she began opening her other dresser drawers surveying her clothing. What was she going to do about a wardrobe now that she had a job which didn't require a uniform? Her inventory was sad and worn looking. With her first paycheck she'd make a trip to the thrift shop and hoped there'd be something decent. The thought of having to spend some of the little bit of money she had, nearly put her over the edge. She'd table the thought for the next day. After all, why ruin a perfectly nice afternoon?

Chapter 23

EUNICE WAS IN THE KITCHEN making herself a cup of coffee when she heard a rap at her front door. She'd just gotten up and had thrown on her bathrobe and slippers. *Who was at the door at this hour of the morning? Certainly not Moxie,* Eunice thought. Moxie had gotten so relaxed at Eunice's, she often popped in the back door and called in to Eunice rather than knocking every time she appeared. It made Eunice very happy Moxie was feeling more and more comfortable with their relationship.

Eunice swiftly walked through the house to the front door and peaked out through the sidelight window running vertically adjacent to the large, heavy mahogany door. A silhouette shifted. She reached for the knob and flipped the deadbolt lock. When she opened the door, a policeman standing with his back to the door looking out at her front lawn, turned around and faced Eunice.

Whatever could he want? Oh dear God, I hope Moxie

is all right, Eunice thought, wrapping her bathrobe tightly around herself, and synching up the belt.

"Good morning, Officer. Can I help you?"

"I hope so," said the ruddy-faced gentlemen, "I'm Officer Hogan. I'm here to talk with you about the fire late yesterday afternoon."

"Fire? Oh, dear, I didn't hear any sirens." Eunice's thoughts instantly traveled to her guest cottage. Panic hit her immediately. She paled and caught the door knob trying to steady herself.

"Probably not. You're a bit too far from the donut shop down on Prospect Street to have heard the fire engines go out."

"The Donut Shop on Prospect burned yesterday?"

"Yes, sometime after 2:00 p.m., shortly after closing the place caught fire. We're trying to determine the cause, and we're interviewing people who frequent the place who might know something or may have seen something. Matt, the manager, gave me your name and said you're a regular customer. That's why I've come to speak with you."

"Is it suspicious?"

"That's what we're trying to determine," said Officer Hogan. "It was a total loss. It will take us a while to put the pieces together and determine what the accelerant was and where the fire originated. Thankfully it was after hours, and there were no injuries or lives lost. "

"Oh, my! That's awful. My Toby's not going to like that. We're going to have to find a new place to get his chocolate donuts. I hope he's not going to be too picky and have me running all over the city to find some that can measure up!"

"When was the last time you visited the place, ma'am?"

"Why, yesterday. I stopped in just before closing and picked up some chocolate donuts for my Toby."

"You notice anything unusual?"

Eunice thought for a minute. "Not really. It was like any other day. Matt was there and a few other of the regulars."

"How about the servers?"

"Well, Moxie waits tables most mornings but, she wasn't there. Some new girl I'd never seen before helped me." Eunice thought back to the day before. It did seem odd Moxie wasn't there because she'd sworn the young woman had said she was on the schedule. It's one of the reasons Eunice decided to drive into town in the first place. Even though she'd never said as much to Moxie, as Eunice got to know the young woman better she thought of herself as her guardian. The poor dear girl needed someone to watch out for her. Eunice could tell how alone Moxie felt in the world by just looking at her deportment. Just seeing her a few minutes nearly every day did Eunice's heart good, and she'd hoped it made a difference in the life of the young woman by helping her to feel as if someone cared about her well-being.

"Since you're a frequent customer at the donut shop, is there anything, anything at all, you've heard that's concerning? I know how in places like that regulars get their earful of local gossip. They get to know the employees and hear of workplace disputes and the like."

Eunice thought for a minute. "I can't say I've heard or seen anything questionable. I will say though from talking to Moxie she's always said the place needed a good fire. I mean… she said Matt, the manager is a real nice guy and seems to run a good operation. But the fryer for the donuts isn't exactly well-ventilated. The place is old and crusty with a buildup of grease. I'd take my business elsewhere, but Toby likes their donuts. Matt is an awful nice guy and helpful in the community. I like supporting his business."

"This Moxie you just told me about—what do you know about her?" The cop leaned in closer as if ready to take in an earful.

"Actually, she lives in my guest cottage. Poor dear. She was living out on the streets, and I've given her a place to live down at my little studio apartment. She's had some struggles throughout her life… like other stories I'm sure you've heard before—moved from foster home to foster home. Sometimes it leaves its mark."

"Did you see Moxie yesterday?" asked Officer Hogan.

"Well, no, actually I didn't. She said she was on the schedule, that's why I went down to the donut shop in the first place. I like to keep tabs on her. She's so alone in this world. So, every couple of days I check in on her either by stopping in her place of work or stopping in to my guesthouse to take her a little something to eat or I'll invite her here."

"When was the last time you saw her?"

"Oh Officer, Moxie might be a loner but she means no harm. She's a good person."

"So, when was the last time you saw her?"

"The day before yesterday. I picked her up. She was on her way home from work." Suddenly Eunice thought about how strange it was she saw Moxie walking home about a half an hour after her shift started and picked her up. Walking all the way to work for a half an hour of work seemed rather ridiculous. Where was the sense in that? It seemed to Eunice Matt should have better planned his employee's schedule. But Moxie didn't seem phased by it so Eunice kept her mouth shut and didn't pry.

"Thank you very much for your time, ma'am. Is your guest house the little place I saw at the beginning of your driveway?"

"Yes, Officer, it is."

"I think I'll stop by on my way out and have a chat with your tenant." Officer Hogan turned around and headed for the police car.

Eunice watched him drive off, turned, went inside and closed and locked the front door.

"Toby, dear, come here. Mommy has some sad news to tell you. And please don't say I told you so! I'd defend Moxie till the end, if I had to."

Chapter 24

"HELLO, MILDRED SPEAKING."

"Hi Mildred, it's me, Moxie."

"Oh, how are you? What a nice surprise to hear your voice." Mildred could count on one hand the number of times they'd talked on the phone.

"I wanted to warn you. You might get like…a visit like from a policeman."

"A policeman? Are you okay Moxie? Has something happened?" Mildred asked, the blood draining from her face.

"It's about the fire down at the donut shop, my old place of employment."

"Fire? What fire?"

"Evidently, sometime yesterday, shortly after closing, the place like… went up in smoke. A few hours ago a policeman, I think he said his name was Officer Hogan, stopped by my apartment and questioned me. He said it's routine. They're talking to people who frequent the place and employees to see if anyone saw anything out of place or suspicious.

It burned to the ground and they are trying like… to piece things together.

Mildred had heard Moxie say a number of times the place needed a good fire but, my goodness! By now, Mildred thought she knew the girl well enough to know she was not an arsonist and had no grounds for setting fires to any place. She was just not that kind of person. That's why Mildred had worked on Moxie's behalf to get her a new job at the sewing shop. She deserved more than a job with no future at a donut shop.

But, you never know what's in people's minds. Especially when they get their backs up about something, thought Mildred, that's why she'd been so careful in getting to know her. Mildred had a sneaking suspicion yesterday's hiring came at just the right time. Moxie hadn't said as much, but after talking with Eunice the day before yesterday, it seemed Moxie was out of a job.

Dear God! Moxie wouldn't have torched the place in retribution if she was fired, would she? What was the truth of the matter? Why else would Moxie go into work for only a half an hour and then turn all the way around and go back home again, unless, she'd been fired or sick. It was too long of a trek. But, Eunice said when she saw Moxie on the side of the road headed home from work so early in the morning, she looked fine. When she picked her up, she didn't mention not feeling well. She seemed to be in her right mind and she didn't seem nervous or anxious.

"So, the policeman wanted to know my whereabouts yesterday afternoon," said Moxie. "I told him I was with you. You came over to my house about 10:00 a.m. and then you drove me over to the sewing shop around 10:45 or 11:00 o'clock so I could talk with the manager about my new job. Then I was at your place having lunch and visiting for the rest of the afternoon. About four-thirtyish you drove me home."

"That's a fact!" said Mildred, thinking back to the day before. She thought as they were visiting in the living room after the dishes were done, she'd heard the fire trucks go out. If she had to guess it was probably about 3:00 o'clock but she really hadn't paid much mind.

Knowing the young woman couldn't have been involved made Mildred feel much better. She'd made mistakes before about people's character. From everything she'd seen, Moxie seemed like an upstanding person. Who doesn't have rough patches in life, the elderly woman pondered and a child's uprooted family was never their fault.

Chapter 25

Moxie had no sooner opened her eyes and her phone rang. "Hello?" she said in a sleepy voice.

"Good morning, sunshine, what are you doing today?" asked a cheery voice. It was Eunice, her landlady.

"I'm not sure," said Moxie groggily.

"Say, I could use a hand today. I found some more stuff I need to go through, and I am wondering if you could help me."

More stuff? How could Miss Eunice have more stuff? What was it now the old lady wanted to go through? It was kind of fun helping her sort through her things but Moxie had other plans in mind like turning over and going back to sleep. The guilt got the better of her when she once again thought how kind it was for Miss Eunice to give her a place to live free of charge. "Sure, I can help you out today, Miss Eunice. Moxie looked at the time on her cellphone. "How about 10:30ish?"

"Splendid. That's fine. It will give me time to go

for a little walk with my Toby. See you in a little while."

Moxie hopped out of bed and headed for the bathroom. Her shower thoughts were of the possibilities of an increased paycheck once she started her new job. Perhaps, she thought, she'd be able to afford more variety in her diet in the future.

"Thanks for coming over today, Sweetie Pie. Let's go up into the spare bedrooms and haul out the boxes and bags in the closets and go through them."

Am I losing it or what? Moxie thought. *Hadn't she already done that?*

The two women went up the stairs and into one of the bedrooms. When Miss Eunice opened the closet doors, black plastic bags tumbled out onto the floor. One by one they began going through the bags making piles. Moxie didn't know much about the value of old clothing or about fancy labels but it seemed some of the items were quite valuable. "Miss Eunice, what are you going to do with all this clothing?" Miss Eunice looked at Moxie who had on the same pair of worn jeans and stained shirt since the last time she saw her.

"I'm not sure dear. Could you use any of them?"

"Well, yes." She needed clothes for her new job badly. She'd seen a bunch of clothing as they went through other bags when paired with the right blouse, top or blazer would make them look better.

For someone who enjoyed mixing and matching styles, they'd be perfect. Or with a little creativity they could even be restyled if someone knew how to sew. Well, that person was not her since she had never put her hands on a sewing machine. But maybe in the future. Long term opportunities were possible with her new job which made her feel hopeful rather than negative and depressed.

"Moxie, I need to make some phone calls. Why don't you continue going through the bags. Pick out whatever you can use."

Perfect! Moxie thought. With Miss Eunice gone from the room, she could really spread things out and put some thought into which items of clothing she might wear. There was such an assortment of styles and sizes. Some were current fashions with price tags still on them from top department stores.

Women! Moxie thought, as she went through the clothing with tags on them, *They buy clothes, get them home and then decide they don't want them for whatever reason—the color is wrong or they don't fit right or don't like them as much as when they were trying them on. Why hadn't they been returned?* For the first time in her life, she really thought about the term "one man's trash is another's treasure."

The oddest thing was the number of vintage-type handkerchiefs among the clothing. Moxie had a vague memory of a book she had once read about how Victorian women were given items of apparel such as fans, gloves, and handkerchiefs as objects of "love tokens" from their suitors. By the number of hankies in the bags it sure appeared Miss Eunice had had her fair share of admirers throughout her life. Many of the handkerchiefs were threadbare.

Moxie looked at her watch. It was already 2:30 p.m. Three hours had passed since Miss Eunice went downstairs she was so absorbed in what she was doing. She would have liked to have stayed all day but her stomach was growling. Whatever Eunice had going in the kitchen smelled delicious. In her rush to get over to her landlord's, she had forgotten to eat something.

During the hours she spent going through bags, Moxie reflected how one's life story could nearly be pieced together by one's personal accumulations. But, how did a rag doll, a handful of children's Golden Books, a sock monkey, a "Lamb Chop" puppet and children's "Learn to Sew Lace Up Cards" Moxie came across fit into the overall picture of Eunice's life? Moxie continued to rummage pondering how her duffel bag of personal possessions told the entire tale of her existence with one brief word—pitiful!

Just as she was considering heading home, Moxie came across a black and white photo, smaller than a snapshot, of a woman and a little girl standing posed, holding hands. Moxie glanced briefly, put it back in the bag and continued sorting. Suddenly she realized something in the picture captivated her but she wasn't sure what. She dug the photo back out of the bag and stared at it closer. Suddenly she felt woozy, her stomach constricted and she felt like she might throw up. Trying to avoid vomiting, she took several deep breaths to calm herself. When the nauseous feelings subsided and to take her mind off of what was upsetting her, she thought about how grateful she felt she was in a sitting position. Had she been standing, she would have keeled over when she came to an abrupt realization after seeing the picture.

Eunice's footsteps were audible on the staircase. Quickly Moxie stuffed the photo in the black bag of clothing she had selected to take home.

"Have you found some clothing you like?" Eunice asked as she walked into the bedroom. "Oh, my, you don't look so well, dear. Is everything alright? What is it? You're looking rather sallow."

"Ummm...I'm just feeling a little low on energy. I'm okay. I just realized I haven't really eaten today." Moxie tried to gather herself, clasping her hands together to stop them from shaking. She cleared her throat. "Oh, Miss Eunice, I forgot to tell you something important!" Moxie said, trying to regain her composure and sound cheerful, "I have a new job starting next week. I really could use some of these clothes. Gone is the waitress uniform."

"Oh, really dear. How wonderful! What is it you will be doing?"

"I've gotten a job in a sewing shop down on Commerce Street.

"Terrific! I think I know something about the store. I've been in it a time or two before."

"There were some brand new items of clothing with like… tags still on them. Did you know they were in those bags? Are you sure you don't like… want them?"

"What use are they to me? They don't fit, so you

may as well get use out of them if you like them and if they fit you."

Moxie had quickly slipped on a couple of the items and looked at them in the full length mirror on the back of the bedroom door. She found not only did they fit, she loved them. And they were more current in style than many of the others. In fact, it was strange. They were nothing like the clothing she had seen the old lady wear before. The clothes were trendier, styled for younger women. "You don't know how much I appreciate this clothing, Miss Eunice!"

"I think I do dear. Do you want to wrap things up for today and head on home?"

"I'd love to stay longer but I have some things to do this afternoon since I start my job on Monday." Just then Moxie's stomach let out an enormous growl.

"Okay, but don't be shy. Whenever you have free time, there are lots more bags and boxes to go through, but at least you have some clothing to get you started. And you were a big help today, I really don't enjoy sorting through old clothing." The two women proceeded down the stairs into the kitchen.

As Moxie neared the back door to leave, Miss Eunice opened her refrigerator and took out a brown paper bag with twisted raffia handles and handed it to her. Stamped across the bag was a quote, "Tote your heart and share it, wherever you go."

"Here dear, take this home. I made this while you were upstairs. There is way too much. Toby and I will never eat all this stew. From the sound of your stomach talking to you and your pasty appearance

I think you need it. I want you to have this for your apartment too, I've been growing it for years. Her landlady handed Moxie a small glass terrarium shaped like a small house, with ivy and moss growing in it.

These plants and clothing, consider them an early birthday present. It's fun to watch the intermingling of life within the little abode."

"Oh, what a neat terrarium. Thanks so much!"

Eunice waved her hands as if to say "Oh, it's nothing dear." But to Moxie it meant so much to get a little gift. How could her landlady know her birthday was coming up? Moxie had never mentioned it. She thought back to how many of her birthdays had never really been acknowledged.

With her hands laden with a bag full of clothing and a second bag with a sizeable container of beef stew and potted plants, Moxie walked back to her apartment. Once inside, she set the terrarium down and closely studied the plantings. Much to her surprise there was a fern frond poking its head through the green moss. She also discovered a miniature rusted iron cross planted among the moss, barely visible. The trailing ivy had nearly overtaken it. *How cool!* Moxie thought. She knew she'd get pleasure from watching the tender fern springing up and the other plants growing inside the terrarium.

Moxie hung some of the clothing which needed no alteration in her closet. She drew the black and white photo out of the bag and sat for a few minutes studying it intensely. Upon further inspection, there was no doubt what she saw.

Opening her sock and underwear drawer, she reached to the back corner. She put the black and white photo in the tissue that wrapped the bracelet and the unattached cross.

She stuffed what remained in the bag under the futon to go through later when she could give it full attention.

Moxie got a whiff of the beef stew and suddenly became ravenous. Her mouth watered. She knew she needed to eat so she headed into the kitchen.

Miss Eunice's generosity was more than plenty to warm and fill her belly. She'd noticed it was getting much colder in her apartment in the evening, and the woodstove, her only source of heat, had so very little wood beside it she hadn't dared to use it. She was saving it for even colder nights.

Chapter 26

It had been a whirlwind of a week. What with starting a new job, and getting used to her new schedule, the time went quickly. Moxie felt as if she had so much to learn before she could really be helpful to customers. She hung onto Meredith's every word.

Sometimes so Mildred didn't have to make a trek over to pick-up Moxie, Eunice gave her a lift to the sewing shop. Between the two older women, getting to work was not the problem Moxie thought it'd be. Walking the distance wouldn't have been possible. She was relieved her days of walking the railroad track into town were over.

In their travels, Mildred subtly hinted to the young woman Meredith expected her employees to go to work looking presentable. Her days of throwing on a pair of jeans and her ratty corduroy jacket were over. Moxie was very grateful Eunice had given her some pass-along clothes and she took a lot of pleasure putting together her wardrobe; laying her clothes out the night before. It made it easier if she already knew what she was going to wear in the morning, rather than trying to put together an outfit just before leaving for work.

As Moxie helped Mrs. Wilson close up shop at the end of her first week, Meredith turned and said, "I love seeing you come in the door every morning! You are so beautifully put together. You inspire me with your outfits."

I inspire you? Yeah, right! The young woman thought her boss was just being nice.

"Yes, I am serious. I mean it. You do! If you use your talent for color and design to the fullest we sure will have some beautiful creations coming out of this shop in the future. You've made remarkable progress this week in remembering the types of fabrics we have in store. Next week we will concentrate on learning some of the sewing accessories and their purpose. It will take a while; there is a lot to learn in the Notions Department. By the way, please don't forget on Monday the basics quilting class begins at 6:00 p.m. Do remember to pack something for dinner. I'll be leaving at 5:00 p.m. on Monday, so let's go over the closing procedure once again. It will be up to you to close up shop on Monday after class at 8:00 p.m."

Wow, thought the young woman, *she must really like… trust me!*

"And before we leave today, you need to go over to the remnants area and pick out fabric for the small wall hanging you'll be learning to make in the quilting class. Remember, it's one of the perks of the job. Free remnants for anything you wish to sew."

Meredith hadn't mentioned that when she was hired. The starting pay wasn't that great, but the perks… not too shabby!

Before they closed up for the day, Moxie enjoyed picking out material and putting together a colorful assortment of fabrics to include in her first project. She'd seen the pattern of the wall hanging project and chose a mix of small floral patterns in soft blues and greens along with a few solids in the same hues and values. She figured she'd hang on to her first quilting project for a long, long time if it turned out well. So she selected colors that wouldn't get on her nerves. Moxie was beginning to feel more in tune with herself, her relationships and with her world than she ever had before. She was gradually getting to understand the meaning of a quote she once read by Antoine de Saint Exupery, *"True happiness comes from the joy of the zest of creating new things."*

There had been another positive development greatly relieving some of Moxie's stress. One evening Eunice called and said to look for a delivery of wood next to her doorstep when she returned home from work the next day. "It will be up to you, dear, to stack it up."

"That's fine. I'm so grateful for your help it's the least I can do." And Moxie wholeheartedly meant it. She hadn't yet received her first paycheck, and she had no idea where she was going to get money to buy wood for the wood stove to heat her place. The delivery was very welcomed.

The following evening, when she returned home

from work several cords of wood were waiting to be piled. Thankfully, the logs were cut into just the right sizes for the woodstove, and of manageable weight. There were even some thin branches good for kindling. A few of the leaves hadn't completely dried and the contrast between the white bark and golden leaves was pretty. Magnificent, actually. After she'd had a bite to eat, she turned on the exterior lights and set to work neatly making a mountain of wood outside her door and a small pile beside the woodstove.

Over the next few evenings, Moxie enjoyed the physical labor. As she stacked the aspen logs, she saw something else she had never noticed before. The bark of the aspen had what looked like "eyes" staring back at her. It was a little eerie. Yet, she knew her labor was proof of something good and uplifting. Even though it was hard to express what she was feeling perhaps well-being and fulfillment, like she yet to experience, were apt descriptions.

Chapter 27

As the afternoon went on, Moxie became more anxious. She'd only been working at the fabric shop for a week, and Meredith expected her to hold down the place and close up shop for the first time after the quilting class was over. Five o'clock rolled around and Meredith, left for home. Moxie locked up the store as instructed.

Moxie had thirty minutes to kill before Ms. Easterbrook, the quilting teacher, was supposed to arrive at the store. She sat on a stool in the backroom eating leftover pizza Miss Eunice had brought over the evening before. Eunice said she and Toby couldn't finish it because he had gotten into the chocolate donuts she'd left sitting on the cocktail table. She'd found a new place to frequent and Toby liked their donuts even better. She said she didn't dare give him much pizza for fear he'd "upchuck." *What a word,* Moxie thought. Someone else she knew used it instead of saying "throw up" but she couldn't think who.

At precisely 5:30 p.m. a rap came on the back door in the stockroom. Moxie unlocked the door and peered out, figuring it was the teacher. Instead, she came face to face with Eunice.

"Miss Eunice, whatever are you doing here?"

"I'm here for the quilting class."

"Oh, I didn't know you were attending. I hadn't yet looked at the names on the enrollment list. So you want to learn how to quilt, too?"

Eunice chuckled. "I'm actually the teacher."

"The teacher?" She had no idea Miss Eunice's last name was Easterbrook. When they'd met, Miss Eunice introduced herself without her last name and Moxie never thought to ask her what it was.

To think at her age Miss Eunice still continued to work was surprising. From the look of her property—her large house filled with accumulations and her ranch lands with the guest house, work was not a necessity.

"I had no idea you had a job!"

"Oh no, dear, I don't consider this my job. It's my passion. I've been teaching sewing for as long as I can remember. It's what keeps me going. I could no longer continue to man the store so I hired Meredith. It became too hard to be on my feet all the time. But I won't let go of my sewing classes until I'm ready to keel over.

"You like… own the store?"

"Let's just say I still have a partial interest in it."

"Well, what can I do to help you get ready for the workshop?"

"Let's get out the folding chairs. Set up a dozen. Thanks for pitching in so we'll be ready in time." The two women set to work. The teacher obviously had prepared for this class many times over she was so organized, quite unlike her home.

At 5:45 p.m. as instructed by her boss, Moxie unlocked the store door. When the dozen participants arrived she checked off their names on her handwritten list. For the next two hours, it was as if Moxie was spellbound. Except for during her high school art classes, she had never been so engrossed in learning. The class discussed some of the basic tools needed for hand quilting such as templates, hoops, and types of batting. It was a great way to learn more about her job and what she already hoped someday would become her real passion.

After the workshop and after the store was buttoned up tight, Moxie hitched a ride home with Miss Eunice. Their conversation in the car was easy and relaxed.

"So, how's the new job going?"

"I like it already, it feels so good to work at something that interests me. I haven't felt so happy since.....well, since... I don't know when." Moxie knew when, but she hated to rehash her previous life. She was moving forward in a positive direction. What she wanted to say was "Since I lived four years with the foster mother who made me feel loved and adored."

As they drove along, Moxie thought about how

nice it was Mildred happened to show-up for the class also. It was a little puzzling though the way Mildred wrote in her spiral notebook throughout the entire class time.

Chapter 28

THE DAYS PASSED BY QUICKLY FOR MOXIE. She was learning so much at her new job, and she had participated in any extra workshops the shop offered in the evening. With time, she realized what a gift she had been given living so closely to Eunice. The older woman had become her mentor in more ways than one and any spare time was spent over at Eunice's learning how to use a sewing machine. Moxie was a quick study absorbing everything like a sponge.

One day Moxie came home from work and was surprised to find a box in the middle of the floor in the living area of her apartment. There were no clues or markings on the exterior as to what was inside it. She opened it up and found a sewing machine, which was not new, but not an antique either. Looking it over, Moxie noticed there were many features she needed to learn about. At the bottom of the box was a notecard that simply said, "Enjoy! Create! Learn! Love, Toby" There was also a bag with spools of thread in every color under the rainbow, a shiny pair of shears, a pin cushion, a seam ripper, a measuring tape and a few other basic notions she'd need for any sewing project.

Several days previously when she was helping Miss Eunice clean out yet another bedroom closet, she found bags and bags of remnants of fabric. "Do you want them?" the old lady asked. "All these years of owning a fabric shop I've accumulated so much. But, I couldn't bear to part with any of it. Something has been telling me I'll find the right person to pass the fabric along to. And I believe I have."

"That makes me feel good, Miss Eunice. It means more than you will ever know."

"I think I understand, dear." Miss Eunice went over and hugged her. "Now, do you want the fabric?"

"I'd love it! I'd hate to see the fabric go into the trash." That evening the aspiring seamstress took the bags of material home with her. When she rummaged through the bags, her mind went on an incredible journey thinking of so many things she could create with the fabric. The possibilities were endless.

And now she had the tool she needed to begin stitching. Moxie sat staring at the sewing machine in disbelief. A phone call to thank Toby just wouldn't do. She still hadn't met this Toby character but needed to thank him in person. Perhaps he was just a "fig newton" of Miss Eunice's imagination, as she suspected. She was determined to find out. Where had she gotten that expression? She didn't remember but it made Moxie laugh every time she thought of it. It was funny how certain memories and phrases stuck with a person. Especially little insignificant things.

She took off down the long driveway to Miss Eunice's house and knocked on the door. After a short delay the door opened.

"I'm sorry to stop by without calling first. Is Toby here?"

Oh, Mother of God, what am I going to tell her? thought Eunice. "Ummmm.... Why no, dear, he isn't here. When I chastised him for knocking over my chocolate martini again last night he had a little hissy fit, and took off. He'll be back, I'm not worried. I know he'll want his chocolate ice cream before bedtime."

"Well, I came to thank him for the sewing machine. I am so excited and wanted to say thanks in person, rather than on the telephone. It was beyond kind for him to give the sewing machine to me!"

"Toby and I thought you might like to have it. I'll tell him you came over to thank him personally. It's just one more thing taking up space in the attic. This way, you can sew at your leisure and not have to come over to my house. But, please do me a favor. Just because Toby's given you the sewing machine, don't make yourself a stranger. It's my pleasure to pass what I know as a fabric artist along to you. I so enjoy our time together." She patted Moxie's arm gently.

Moxie hugged Miss Eunice goodbye and headed back to her apartment. She couldn't wait to set up the sewing machine on the table in the small kitchenette area and get started on a project. She knew exactly what she wanted to sew. She knew she'd better set up shop close to the Mister Coffee® Miss Eunice had given her explaining, "He was just sitting in the attic, doing nothing. Toby said you ought to have him and put him back to work." Moxie was glad to put Mr. Coffee® into service. Many late nights were ahead with her projects.

Chapter 29

IT HAD BEEN TWO YEARS since Moxie was hired by Sew the Heart, the name she suggested when Miss Eunice, the co-owner, and Meredith, the manager, decided it was time to invest in the future by giving the shop an overhaul. They changed the name of the company to bring it current with what people were looking for in creative business.

Time and time again she had proven to Meredith and Eunice she was reliable and a natural when it came to fiber arts and to entrepreneurship in general. Moxie had used her technology skills to set up an inventory system on the computer to track the fabric and the multitude of sewing accessories in the shop. She'd been rewarded for her efforts with several raises. She also received a small consulting fee at the end of each month. Often when a repeat customer came in the door of the shop looking for guidance on picking out fabric and colors, they asked for Moxie. She, in turn, received a small percentage of the sale. *Every little bit helps,* Moxie thought. Her finances were looking up. It felt good to be relieved of financial pressures, and it helped Moxie's outlook tremendously.

She thought it was wise Miss Eunice had sold off some of her things taking up space in the attic and invested the money into upgrades for the business. Many of the valuable antiques were just collecting dust. Other stuff was put in the corner of the basement waiting for who knew what.

As her income increased Moxie offered to begin paying rent for the guest cottage apartment, but Eunice wouldn't hear of it. She said Moxie's help at her house was more than payback. One day, Moxie bought the most affordable, user-friendly computer she could find on the internet. She had been saving money towards it and took it over to Miss Eunice as a surprise. She showed her elderly landlord the basics of using a computer, and how to use online banking. "Teaching her that," said Eunice, "made Moxie worth more than all her weight in silver."

Moxie had taken it upon herself to make other small improvements to the store like sewing some small three-by-three foot quilt samples with various palettes of colors that looked well together. It made identifying customers preferences so much easier, and they looked pretty displayed on the walls. She could relate to the overwhelming feelings that came to new customers when they walked in and saw such a vast assortment of colors and patterns. This way, customers could see samples of pastels, primary colors, earthy tones, or hues of darker colors and identify their preferences. Some people liked all solid colors and others a mix and match approach to their design incorporating solids, stripes, patterns and floral fabric.

Moxie had also suggested something which seemed rather unconventional at first to Meredith and Eunice but when they saw the success of the program, they couldn't dispute it. Her little seed of an idea was bringing like-minded people in the door and spreading joy.

Every few months, they invited a speaker to do some evening talks about art, crafts, and creativity regarding its relationship to happiness and personal fulfillment. The women had cleared a little corner of the store and put in a few antique chairs from Miss Eunice's attic where customers could relax and visit. With time, shoppers were congregating longer and purchasing more because they had found friendship and fellowship in their joint craft interests. Free coffee and tea was always available to encourage them to stay. "Please don't put out hot chocolate because it makes such a mess," requested Eunice. Although Moxie didn't understand how instant, powdered hot chocolate made any more of a mess than coffee or tea, who was she to question the store owner?

One day Eunice admitted to Moxie her way of doing business was from the dinosaur age. "Moxie, you came along just when we really needed you. It was time to either close up shop or invest in the future. I'm happy we went with option #2. Things are looking up."

Granted Moxie was new to business, and didn't have a wealth of experience like her superiors, but for God's sake, she thought, *How have you operated this way for so long?*

Chapter 30

MOXIE FELT SURE HER INTEREST IN FABRIC ARTS was her future, and she couldn't learn quickly enough. It all takes time, she tried to assure herself. Masters at a craft are not made overnight; it's a life-long learning process.

With each passing month, she learned more about the art of sewing and began to incorporate as many beautiful details as possible into the pillows she was crafting in her spare time for her two elderly friends. She wanted to have something to be really proud of when she gave gifts from her heart.

On one of her days off, Moxie knocked on Miss Eunice's door hoping she'd be home so the sewing whiz could show her on her fancy sewing machine, with a pleating foot, how to finish off the border of a pillow with piping and a gathered ruffle of eyelet lace. No one answered. She cocked her head sideways and put her ear up to the closed door trying to listen for the sound of footsteps. When she heard nothing, she knocked again even louder. Eunice slowly opened the door. Although it was 11:00 a.m., Eunice was still dressed in her pale pink chenille robe and Dearfoam© slippers. She had dark circles under her eyes and looked as if she'd had a rough night. Her gray hair, which was usually beautifully coiffed, looked as if the rats had been nesting in it.

"Come on in," said Eunice, cheerlessly opening the door wider.

"Are you okay?" asked Moxie with concern in her voice.

"I feel like I'm going to upchuck at any moment," and her friend ran off to the bathroom.

Moxie sat at the kitchen table waiting. She heard the toilet flush and thought perhaps she should have called before she came over.

The old woman walked out of the bathroom, shuffled into the kitchen and took a seat. She put her elbows on the table and held her head up with both hands. She looked dreadful and her skin had a sallow tone to it.

"I think I've caught you on a bad day. I was going to ask for your help with my sewing project but, I don't think this is a good time."

Eunice reached into the pocket of her well-worn bathrobe and took out a yellowed embroidered cloth handkerchief and wiped under her eyes.

"It's okay, dear, I'm just in mourning."

"Oh, I'm sorry, Miss Eunice. I didn't realize…." Moxie didn't quite know what to say to her friend. She hadn't previously mentioned anyone who was ill or dying.

"It's Toby. I'm so over him even though I'll miss him terribly. He's been with me for a long time. I'll be okay. We had our final celebration last night and no more chocolate martinis, forever." She swallowed hard and took a deep breath as if to get control of her emotions. "But, things have changed, and I have to remind myself I no longer need him. I now have a new companion in my life and her name is Moxie. With your forgiveness, my life will become much richer." She wiped her eyes again.

Moxie sat quietly listening; it's all Moxie knew what to do as a friend. She wasn't quite sure what Miss Eunice meant by having Moxie's forgiveness but she thought she might have an idea.

"Did her friendship really mean that much to the elderly woman?" If so, then the feelings were mutual. Moxie really had come to love this lady who had taken her in and given her a place to live and even more. Besides being a mentor, Eunice had become her confident, a mother of sorts, a faithful encourager and a soulmate all wrapped up in one beautiful package.

Miss Eunice continued, "It was time to let Toby go. He wasn't good for me anyway. He made me eat too many chocolate donuts and drink too many chocolate martinis. And then before we went to bed, every night he insisted we eat chocolate ice cream. Last night, he stole the chocolate ganache cake from the freezer I was saving for a special occasion and ate it frozen along with his chocolate ice cream. I told him a few weeks ago when he upchucked all over my oriental rug, 'Jesus, Mary and Joseph, Toby, eating all this *food of the gods* has got to stop! If it's *the food of the gods*, for Christ sake, give it back.' I'm tired of being controlled by it....eerr, umm, I mean I'm tired of seeing Toby being controlled by his chocolate, morning, afternoon and night." Eunice let out a big sigh.

"But no, Toby, he wouldn't listen. Now, look," Eunice, inhaled deeply, "it's come to this! I've had to kick him out of the house." She shook her head solemnly. "I told Toby, once he's out of here, no more chocolate will ever be allowed in this house again and that's final, finis, I'm done!" Miss Eunice said with great conviction.

"Oh, I am so sorry. I know Toby meant a lot to you," said Moxie compassionately, playing along, knowing full well what the real story was.

As time went on and as the young woman got to know her landlady much better, she figured out Eunice, in her loneliness, had manufactured in her mind an imaginary friend. Moxie knew something about having an imaginary friend. Hers had helped her in times of stress and heartache. She well understood Toby was only a "fig newton of Eunice's imagination," (albeit a chocolate one!) and he was Eunice's enabler.

Moxie had caught on to Miss Eunice's weakness when she realized the leftover chocolate donuts were not going to the homeless. She was bringing them home to feed just one of her addictions. It was obvious Eunice had had one too many chocolate goodies the night before and finally had come to terms with the fact she had a problem. She was using chocolate as a crutch.

Ah, well, thought Moxie, *addiction to other substances can be much worse.* She knew from experience. And anyway, how much chocolate could a person really eat before they tired of it? As far as she was concerned, the best way to cure an addiction to chocolate was to go work in a donut or candy shop. Just being around the sickening sweet smell continually makes a person nauseous. *Thank God, my days of addiction struggles are over,* pondered Moxie. Now she had a new albatross around her neck—sewing. But at least it was therapeutic.

Moxie stood to leave, taking Miss Eunice's two hands in hers.

"Dear God, Please help Eunice hang on to tight control to keep her lips sealed if she is given any more blessed chocolate. Help her to know chocolate is her enemy and to receive this gift of letting go."

"Amen," the two women said in unison.

"Stay strong, Eunice!" Moxie said, as she left Eunice's house.

The young woman knew she was fortunate. Although she had struggled with different kinds of addiction, compared with many people it was only for a short time. Kicking her habits wasn't quite as hard for her as it was for others. For some it's a lifelong struggle.

She rapidly realized how much better her life had become once she was removed from the drugs and alcohol her "friends" were providing for her. She gradually came to understand the pills Jared had been giving her had become a mechanism for dulling a different kind of pain. Moving to a new place with empty pockets so she couldn't buy what fueled her addiction was the best self-help action Moxie had taken since she became an adult. She wasn't sure why she decided to uproot herself from Kellenville and began to hang around Hopewell. But, it just seemed the right thing to do. Life just twenty miles away in Hopewell was very different.

Once she found God in her heart she was finally really determined to beat her addiction and her life changed for the better. But, healing wasn't just about living in a new town. None of her understanding about addiction would have come to her if Mildred hadn't come into her life. She'd had experience with it, she said, from dealing with her sister. Mildred suggested Moxie go through the twelve step program. Moxie realized no one could tackle her addiction, except herself with a little help from HIM.

That's all past history, Moxie thought. After all what good had come of walking through the pain repeatedly? Her life was on track and nothing was going to derail it. Her future at Sew the Heart was looking healthy. There was no way she'd let herself slip back.

Chapter 31

THE BELL ON THE SEWING STORE DOOR CLANGED, she was certain of it. Looking through the open door which led from the storage room into the shop, Moxie couldn't see who entered, so she headed into the retail space. The words, *"Listen as your day unfolds. Challenge what the future holds,"* pealed out from Moxie's iPad. As soon as she arrived at work, she put on Pandora. ***You Gotta Be*** was among her playlist of tunes, and it rang out loudly.

She was surprised to see it was Mildred who had come into the store. Sitting in the chair adjacent to the cash register counter, her feet moved to the rhythm of the music and she tapped her thighs with her fingers, drumming in time with the music. Moxie quietly watched from a distance. From the smile on the old lady's face, she was obviously enjoying herself.

Mildred rose when the song was over. She saw Moxie and walked over to greet her. "I was listening to the lyrics of that song. Whoever that gal is you are playing on the hi-fi, I like her philosophy."

"That's Des-Ree" said Moxie, as they embraced each other lightly. Mildred held Moxie at arms' length taking in her face and overall appearance.

"You look wonderful. Look at you! When did you cut your hair?"

"About a month ago. I thought it was time for a new "do" to go along with my new life."

It had been six or eight weeks since they'd seen each other. Long gone was Moxie's straggly purple hair with dry, dead ends. Her new chin length hairstyle was extremely becoming and her pierced lip and nose ring were gone too. Mildred was surprised Eunice hadn't said anything about the new cheer in the young woman's voice and the fact her obsession with the word "like" had disappeared from her vocabulary. Now that was progress! *Wasn't it funny how in some cases, time cured all things in young folks,* Mildred thought.

"Mildred, where have you been? I've missed seeing you. Have you been all right?"

"Oh, yes dear, I've just been busy getting our affairs in order. Things we had put off for far too many years are now being taken care of with the lawyers."

"Oh, I don't mean to pry but I hope you aren't having any legal problems."

"Oh no, dear, it's just stuff that's been ignored and now the answers have come. We're putting down everything in writing. It just takes a lot of time and attention. That's all."

Mildred watched Moxie move about the store

tidying it up before the rush of the day began. She noticed even her movements were different. Her head was held higher, she moved with confidence and purpose throughout the store, seeing to it everything was as it should be. She had taken on a sense of ownership in her job. It was delightful to see.

"So, tell me Moxie, fill me in on how things are going for you." It was hardly necessary to ask by her appearance.

She had so much to tell Mildred, such as news of the sewing machine she had "inherited" and about some of the projects she was working on at home in her spare time. "I've been spending a lot of time sewing and creating. It's as if my job and my spare time have all become one. Once I get going on a project, it's hard to stop and go to bed. I get so excited to finish it and see the end result."

"That outfit you have on, did you make it?"

"As a matter of fact I did, in part." Moxie said with a proud look on her face. She was so happy Mildred had noticed. "A couple of months ago, Eunice gave me bags of remnants and bags of dated clothing, and I've been giving new life to them. You know, restyling, repurposing and recycling. I'm hoping someday, I'll have my own label." *Whoops,* Moxie thought. She didn't mean to tell anyone quite yet. She was so excited the news just spilled out of her unexpectedly.

"Well, you've got quite a flair! Your outfit is smashing, and to think you've made it yourself. It's beautifully crafted and you couldn't have chosen a spectrum of colors to compliment your skin tone and new hair color any better. Even your jewelry looks great with the outfit."

"Well, the jewelry came from one of the bags of discarded clothing Miss Eunice had given me. Pretty, isn't it?"

"I've seen your light on late into the evening and wondered what you were doing. Now I know! You're one busy girl, what with the store and working on your projects at home. My goodness, you are one enterprising young lady!"

So, thought Moxie, *it was Mildred's pink Cadillac she had been seeing some evenings going past the guest cottage in the direction of Miss Eunice's house.* She wondered why they'd never told her they were such close friends. Whenever they'd had workshops at Sew the Heart there didn't appear to be any special warmth between the two women. They were very cordial, almost business-like with each other. But not real tight, as far as she could tell.

"Moxie, I hate to pry but I want to ask, do you have a social life?"

"Why yes, I've met so many new people at the shop and we all have so many common interests!" Although she hadn't had the companionship of male friends recently and even though many of the women she had met were not her age, she enjoyed their company. At least these "friends" were not into the drinking and drug scene. She'd had enough of that and she was onto something better. Creating a future for herself.

Mildred asked the question about Moxie's dating life because there was a young man she knew who hinted he might be interested in getting to know more about the young woman. She decided she'd better mind her own business and not play the matchmaker. Someday the two young people may have an occasion to come together but she wasn't going to force the issue. She didn't delve into Moxie's romantic interests any further. Lord knows she'd had enough of that in her life and in her old age she had finally learned when to leave well enough alone. What mattered was they'd finally found the right person and she seemed devoted to developing Sew the Heart for her own future. Mildred was feeling very hopeful her legacy was going to grow into an even larger enterprise. She was so relieved when she opened the local paper. She saw they had quickly detected the source of the fire at the donut shop—ancient and faulty wiring in the fryer. The young woman, the potential successor for her business, had not a thing to do with it.

Who would have ever known this was the same girl Mildred had seen sleeping on the park bench a few years ago? When Mildred saw Moxie she had given the "heads up" to Eunice there was something so very familiar about the girl. They decided they'd learn something about her through their longstanding connections in the community. Then when they were sure, the two women agreed it was time to begin planning how to help the young lady. Their desire to help out someone very special, who through little fault of her own had never gotten what she truly deserved weighed heavy. Yes, it was time to once again build the relationships. Mentoring this young woman must be done very carefully and with stipulations. The "chosen one" needed to show commitment by helping herself too and by proving herself for a truly successful outcome.

Chapter 32

It was crazy nearly five years had gone by since Moxie began her job at Sew the Heart. It never ceased to amaze Moxie how in those five years her life had changed for the better. She couldn't imagine ever again working at a job where she couldn't use her creativity.

Moxie had intended to finish the two pillows and gift them to Eunice and Mildred the first year she started the job at the sewing store. But, year after year went by and other projects took priority. The pillows were set aside.

Meredith was still a stable and reliable employee. She handled the day to day operations on the floor of the store well. But, sometimes Moxie felt a little uncomfortable she had moved ahead of Meredith in her position. But at the same time, she knew it was because of her initiatives in helping to bring the store current. Meredith was not as old as Eunice, and she wasn't quite ready to retire. She seemed very content with her position and her responsibilities. The part time employees, mostly high school students, created a revolving door situation. They came and went after short periods because they were young and often moved on to other things—school, new jobs and relocation.

In five short years and with a lot of hard work and dedication, Moxie had grown her reputation as a design consultant in the fabric arts industry. She started with clients who were looking for advice and help for their home sewing projects and gradually expanded to include commercial design ventures. She had a very fulfilling arrangement with the co-owner of the store, Eunice, as their in-house design specialist.

Two years into her employment, Meredith, Eunice's tenant in the upstairs apartment over the sewing store moved out. A real blessing. Moxie's sewing projects had taken over the small kitchen space of the guest cottage studio apartment. Moving to the very large apartment over the store solved three problems. The space was large enough for both living space and a substantial studio with room to spread out and grow. It allowed her to work more efficiently and handle large projects.

Her transportation issues were solved since she lived where she worked. Rather than have to sink money into a car, Moxie saved for the day when she'd go into business for herself.

When she moved out of the guest cottage studio apartment and into the apartment above the store, Moxie said to Eunice, "Please, don't cut me any deals that wouldn't be right. You've done enough to get my feet underneath me, and I can't thank you enough."

"Oh, dear, you've gotten it all wrong. You have no idea how indebted I feel toward you for all you have done for me. Now, don't you worry about it for a minute, we are in this venture together. We'll work out a fair deal for both of us."

It was time, Moxie thought, to plan and to do something very special to thank the two women for their influence in her life. Moxie had decided she couldn't compete with all the two women had given her. Over the years she tried to repay what she had been given in her own special way. She was determined to plan a memorable day. She told Mildred and Eunice to save the date!

Over the few years Moxie lived and worked above the store, she had seen a decline in both of her elderly friends. Eunice hadn't come upstairs into the apartment above the store since the day she brought Moxie an antique sampler stitched with the words "Home Sweet Home." Climbing stairs, she said, was getting more difficult and Mildred seemed to stay busy at home more frequently.

Moxie couldn't wait to show Miss Eunice and Mildred the "make-over" she had given the apartment over the sewing shop. It had been an ongoing project with little investments in new paint and fabric to slipcover tired-looking furniture. Gradually the young woman had created or picked up new decorating items here and there at second hand shops. She had to give herself a pat on the back for her "good eye for design" and the real haven she had created for herself. Moxie discovered as she matured, she was a "nester at heart" and had grown more comfortable with being alone as she grew to like herself. Her inner battles had been quelled and a sense of peace about her life had settled within her. *Someday though,* she thought, *maybe she'd like to find a fella.* She was so caught up in her career, finding a mate wasn't at the top of her priority list. She wanted to make sure she was ready because if she became a mother she would never want any child to go through what she had experienced in her childhood—being given up for adoption. Then when that didn't work having to become part of the foster care system.

Moxie loved the warm feelings she had when she came home to the place where she surrounded herself with all the things she loved. A sacred space where Moxie found solace, inspiration and grew a career she was passionate about.

She remembered hearing somewhere churches often painted their doors red signifying a safe haven. She decided when she repainted the entryway to her apartment, red would be an appropriate color. Now she'd grown up and was out of her funk, she was determined to live a fulfilling life. As a kid, she had little experience and faith life could really be like that.

She grew to better appreciate the four years she spent with the wonderful couple rather than feel resentful for having to leave their shelter. She came to understand her gratefulness had nothing to do with the fact that they lived more comfortably than all the others. They made Moxie feel like she deeply mattered. Rehashing her childhood did no good and she worked very hard to stop doing that. As the girl matured into a young woman she realized the broken pieces in other people's lives were not hers to fix. The only life she had reign over was her own.

What a fortunate chain of events had occurred when she met Eunice on the street the day she gave Moxie a donut. It made her see there are still good people in the world. She'd seen it through her own experience over the past five years. Just when she had almost given up, Eunice came along and helped her when she had nowhere else to go. And Mildred, too. Which reminded Moxie, she still had Mildred's bracelet in her dresser drawer. It had been a long time since she had looked at the fascinating collection of charms, and she vowed to get them out.

Although Moxie would have loved to have attended to every single detail of her special gathering for her elderly friends, she decided to splurge and call a "personal in-home chef." She wanted to give some business back to a chef in town who had sent some referrals Moxie's way by recommending her design services for a new restaurant. *After all,* she thought, *how much would it cost to cater to the needs of three people?* Nothing but the best for her two lady friends, but within reason. Over the years Moxie had learned to carefully budget. She planned the menu with the personal in-home chef paying close attention to the little things that would make the day and the meal so special.

Hiring someone else to tend to the food freed Moxie to finally finish the pillows and spruce up her apartment in anticipation of the party. She planned on lighting scented vanilla candles , and decorating the place with crystal vases of fresh flowers to match her décor. The round dining table she'd set with special care making it as beautiful as the two women she was honoring.

A lot of time was spent finding a perfect little token for each woman to tuck in with the pillows she had custom-crafted. She wrapped them with care, matching the table arrangement. The gifts weren't much compared to all the two women had given Moxie. However, she felt very excited she had found a special, meaningful gift she was proud to give to each one.

She also planned to reveal several epiphanies she'd had. For one, she had come to realize how things accumulate quickly if one is not careful. In the time she lived in Eunice's guest cottage she had gone from owning one bag of possessions to many, many more that needed to be transported when she moved to the space above the sewing store.

Chapter 33

"Come on in ladies, the door is open." Moxie said cheerfully. She'd seen Mildred's pink Cadillac arrive at the store with both women in it. From the window, she watched Miss Eunice use her keys and let them in through the lower delivery area of the store. Moxie paced nervously listening to their chatter back and forth as they slowly climbed the stairs to the apartment.

Moxie quickly took their coats and their bags and stuffed them in the entryway closet, embracing each of the women. "Welcome, dear friend!" The sentiment was returned in kind. All three women were dressed pretty for the occasion in different shades of pink and red. Silver filament earrings shaped like hearts dangled from Eunice's lobes. Mildred had an old fashioned comb in her hair with three pale lilac enamel hearts across it. It fell in pretty with the wave and bluish tint of her gray hair.

Years previously, in one of the bags of clothing her landlord had given her, Moxie had come across a cute pair of red flats with silver hearts clipped to a black bow on the toe along with the best pair of winter boots she'd ever had in her life. The flats were set aside for a special occasion, and there couldn't have been a more appropriate time to wear them.

"Aren't we just stylin' today?" the hostess said to her two lady friends.

"Cheers!" Eunice said when all three had been served wine glasses of sparkling water with raspberries in them. An assortment of appetizers sat on a small cocktail table between the three women —bacon wrapped dates, crab stuffed mushrooms and artichoke heart dip with homemade crostini.

As they ate their appetizers, Moxie noticed both women looking around the room.

"Moxie, the place is gorgeous. Look at this! Your own little sanctuary. It's no wonder you prefer to work upstairs rather than down in the store. I'd find it hard to leave this place too. It's so homey yet, there is a feeling of openness you've created."

"Mildred and I know from experience about finding sanctuaries in all sorts of places and among all sorts of people. Don't we, Mildred?" Mildred nodded her head in agreement.

"I couldn't help but notice the red door. It's so fitting," said Eunice. That was not the only thing the two women noticed. When they entered the apartment they silently pointed out to one another a small rusted iron cross hanging on the red apartment door. It looked so very familiar.

I say it looks nothing like when the previous

tenant, Meredith, had this apartment. Does it Mildred?"

"It was unremarkable, to put it plainly," said Mildred, "but as I told Moxie a while ago, she's got such a flair for decorating."

"Did you see the antique Singer sewing machine foot treadle and base I've incorporated into this side table?"

The two older women ooed and aahed over the piece of furniture, remarking over the clever use of the antique.

"And did you see what's on the wide windowsill over there?" Moxie asked, pointing across the room. The three women crossed the room together.

"Oh, for heaven's sake, Eunice. Look at that, will you. She's turned your old Remington typewriter into a planter box. The inside cavity, where the type keys and ribbon spools were housed, is filled with dirt and succulents.

"Such ingenuity!" the two women said in unison.

Moxie proudly proceeded to point out all of the used furniture both women had given her over the years when they decided to follow the trend of living more simply and with less "stuff." The corner of Eunice's basement where they had been putting household items no longer wanted was now clear.

"I knew I'd find a home for it all somewhere," said Eunice when they brought the last item over to Moxie's apartment and added it to a few furnishings Mildred had given her.

"Eunice, look how well your stuff and mine

mesh together. And Moxie's touches gives it her personality," said Mildred.

"That's why people hire her! She knows how to tie things together! Not everyone can do that." said Eunice.

"Lunch is ready, ladies" said the chef. "Come on over to the table!" The three women walked over.

"This table setting takes my breath away!" said Eunice.

"You went to great lengths today," said Mildred, inhaling all the wonderful smells.

"Oh, it's been fun!" said Moxie. "This is the type of thing I like to do but never really have the opportunity!"

"Yes, dear, I saw that in you a long time ago!" said Eunice as she took a bite of the artfully carved red beets, shaped like hearts on her salad plate.

"Lobster thermidor!" said Mildred, delightedly as she took a bite. "The sauce is out of this world. Why, I don't think I've had lobster thermidor since you and I and Clement and Wilbur took the trip to Maine decades ago. When was that, anyway, Eunice?"

"I don't remember," said Eunice. "A long time before…," Eunice stopped herself short from finishing her sentence.

"So," said Moxie. "You two have known each other for a long, long time."

"Oh dear," said Mildred "we've known each other practically forever. We could write each other's life story!"

"Life story?" questioned Eunice, raising her brow. "I think you should have said saga or melodrama! One of those words would have been more appropriate." For a few minutes, she thought back to the day when the two women met. If it hadn't been for Mildred, Eunice doubted she'd still be around. Mildred was the one who encouraged her to find a hobby she could sink her sorrows into. She began healing by sewing the heart out of her sadness and into happiness and more fulfilling things in her life. So when Moxie suggested they change the name of the store from The Commerce Street Sewing Shop to Sew the Heart both women were all for it. They knew from experience many women would relate to the significance of the name of the business.

The women continued to chat, eat and visit.

"How about we move over to the sofa, and get comfortable," said Moxie when they were finished with their main course. "It's present time. We'll have tea and dessert a little later."

"Sounds like a plan, don't you think Eunice?" asked Mildred.

"You know there is no time like the present, don't you?" said Mildred and Eunice in unison, giggling.

"I never get tired of your wisdom," Moxie said, laughing, looking lovingly first at Eunice and then at Mildred. "It's brought me through a lot."

The three women moved to the living area, and sat down. Eunice looked at the table beside her chair. "Oh, Moxie, I hardly recognize this terrarium, it's grown so much. It looks like it is going to need a larger container."

"It has grown, hasn't it?"

Miss Eunice continued to peer in through the glass walls of the little house. "Oh, look!" you have a third plant, a fern, growing inside the terrarium now. Did you add that?"

"No, the day you gave the terrarium to me, I noticed a little frond poking up through the moss. And it has continued to grow ever since."

"Must have been a latent spore among the moss and the ivy, just waiting for the right conditions to take off. That happens you know," said Eunice. Moxie reflected on what Eunice said.

"The little iron cross planted in the moss, I still have it. I took it out and put it in a more prominent spot. It had become hidden under the ivy." The two older women looked at each other knowing what each was thinking.

"You know, other than our sewing and quilting workshops, I think I could count on one hand the number of times the three of us have been together in the past couple of years. It's usually me alone with one of you."

"That's because we always want to be with you by ourselves!" said Eunice and Mildred at the same time. The three women chuckled. Moxie thought about how she never noticed the two elderly women sometimes finished each other's sentences.

"Are you three ready for some tea and dessert now?" asked the chef.

"In about a half an hour we'll try to stuff more food down," said Moxie. "The company has been divine and it's filled me up."

"This is the best Girlfriends' Day ever!" said Eunice.

"Agreed," said Mildred and Moxie. Although Moxie was really thinking, the best is yet to come.

Moxie walked over to the table and picked up the wrapped gifts. She handed one to each woman being very careful to give each the right one.

"You open your present first, Eunice" said Mildred.

"No, you go on first, Mildred," said Eunice.

Moxie sat quietly feeling her heart pounding inside her chest. It mattered deeply that she had gotten it right. Each gift she had created from her heart reflected what she had learned from each woman and about each woman over their five years of friendship.

"All right, if I must. I hate to tear into this package. It's so beautiful." Mildred said opening her gift first. She looked at the present and held her hand to her mouth. "It is beautiful." She studied the heart-shaped pillow front and back which Moxie had been embellished with meaningful quilted images and pretty trims. Beautifully scrolled across the front of the pillow with embroidery floss were the words *"Our deepest wounds surround our greatest gifts."* ~ Ken Page.

"I'm speechless," said Mildred, swallowing hard, thinking how the three women's relationship was like the stitched pillow she held in her hand. Scraps and tatters of each of their lives clipped and sewn together creating the colorful fabric of their friendship.

Mildred found her voice after a few seconds. "I'm so very touched. I don't know quite know what to say."

"Mildred, there is something in the pocket on the front of the pillow especially for you," said Moxie.

"Oh, dear, really, you shouldn't have. You've done too much." Mildred reached into the pocket on the front of the pillow and drew out her charm bracelet. She began looking at each charm as she had done previously each time she held the jewelry. From the quote on the pillow, Mildred knew Moxie had come to realize the charms were not all about good memories. The meaning of the charms went much deeper, and they included symbols of some dark journeys.

Tears ran down her cheeks when she saw Moxie had added a charm of a miniature writing implement, a silver pen, to the bracelet.

"How did she know?" Mildred muttered under her breath, not loud enough for Moxie to hear it.

Mildred continued to look at each of the charms as if taking inventory. Suddenly she made a realization.

"My missing cross! It's back on the bracelet."

"Yes, it had fallen off. I've had it all along and had it reattached for you," said Moxie. You said you weren't the same without the bracelet so I wanted to return it in better shape than I found it."

"The cross was given to me as a gift from Eunice, many difficult miles into our friendship, right Eunice?"

Moxie looked over at Eunice as she nodded in agreement.

"For Lord's sake, Moxie! Christ, Almighty!" said Eunice, suddenly standing up when the chef walked in the room with a silver tray with three plates of strawberry topped cheesecake. "Haven't you got any chocolate martinis on this menu? And why didn't you tell me to bring my own hankie! These crocodile tears are soaking me," Eunice said wiping her eyes with her sleeve.

Mildred and Moxie burst out laughing.

"What a stitch!" said Moxie.

"See what I've had to put up with all my life? Well, nearly, all my life!" said Mildred.

"So, you two are sisters?"

"Let's just say we are all sisters of the heart," said Mildred and Eunice in unison.

Moxie looked back and forth between the two of them looking for common features. *What difference does it make, anyway?* Moxie thought, repeating to herself a quote she had read somewhere, "The bond that links your true family is not one of blood, but of respect and joy in each other's lives."

"Ok Eunice! It's your turn. Open your gift!" said Moxie cheerfully, clapping her hands together. Things had gotten a little too heavy. She was grateful Eunice had lightened things up.

Eunice lifted her gift from her lap and began tearing off the paper ever so gently. She ran her hands over the lace and the other adornment and frills on the heart-shaped pillow, reading the words embroidered on the front of the pillow out loud, "*You have been in my heart all these years. Love, Moxie.*"

A look arose on Eunice's face the young woman had never seen before. Mildred had never seen Eunice so choked up, and said so in a whispered voice to Moxie. "Not even when Toby, her imaginary canine departed."

Ahhhhh....I did get it, thought Moxie, her invisible friend was exactly as I thought.

"There's something in the pocket in the front of your pillow, too, Eunice," said Moxie.

Eunice dug down deep into the inside of the heart shaped pocket. She pulled out a tiny tabletop sterling silver picture frame inscribed with the words, "No more words are needed between two loving hearts." Eunice stared at the wallet-sized, black and white image of a little girl and a woman holding hands.

"You've held onto this picture of me all these years?" Moxie asked. "I couldn't believe it when I found this photograph as I was sorting through your bags."

"I never wanted to give up hope I'd see you again someday," said Eunice trying to choke back more tears. She rose from her chair, and walked over the where Moxie was sitting. She took the young woman's face between both of her hands, "Oh, Moxie! I'm so sorry," she said, looking deep into her eyes, embracing her tenderly. Eunice's warm body made Moxie feel as if she had been wrapped in a thick, puffy quilt.

Moxie softly whispered, "No more words are needed between two loving hearts" into Eunice's ear.

"Now," said Moxie sternly, pulling away "I've spent too much time looking back. I'll have none of that apologizing stuff! I've moved forward and that's what really counts."

Mildred stood and joined Moxie and Eunice in a group hug. The three embraced like they never wanted to let go.

Suddenly Eunice let go, remembering she and Mildred had two gifts they needed to give the hostess. "Mildred, go get Moxie's presents out of the coat closet, will you?"

Mildred obeyed, ran off and came right back with a package that could have competed with Moxie's gift wrapping any day and a black trash bag.

"Mildred and I have a little something for you. It's a project we have been working on together!"

"For me?" She had hoped they wouldn't do this. As far as Moxie was concerned they had given her more than enough—a new lease on life and a future.

"You, my dear, are the first one to see this," said Eunice.

"Other than us," qualified Mildred. "It's been in the making for a couple of years, but we had to keep embellishing and revising it further as time went along."

"Sounds like the pillows I made for you two!" Moxie said, laughing. "What is it?" she asked as she tore off the paper excitedly.

"A book! ***Coming Home: Helping Others Find***

their Way. By Mildred Millicent, Co-authored by Eunice Easterbrook."

"Look inside, look inside!" said Eunice, as if she was about to burst.

Moxie opened the cover and looked at the signed and personalized title page. "Dear Moxie, Your name couldn't fit you any better. Even as a young child, we knew you had what it takes. Love always, Eunice and Mildred."

A broad smile rose on her face, as Moxie leafed through the pages, reading some of the chapter titles. She realized the book was about two saints, Eunice and Mildred, who had mentored many struggling women over the years getting them started in business. She was their latest star.

"Well, Mildred," said Eunice, I suppose we ought to head on home. This day has been like a dream. I'll look back on it for many years and wonder if it was for real or...." Mildred's voice trailed off.

"If it was just a fig newton of the imagination," Moxie ended the thought.

"Wait a minute you two, don't end the day so quickly," Mildred said, standing, we have one more detail we need to tend to.

"Moxie, go over and sit on the sofa next to Eunice." Moxie stood up from where she was sitting and moved to the sofa. Eunice changed positions until she was sitting smack up against Moxie. The elderly woman gently placed her hand on her young friend's forearm. Mildred set the bag on the sofa on the other side of Moxie.

Moxie opened the bag and peered in. One by one she lifted a rag doll, a handful of children's Golden Books, a sock monkey, a "Lamb Chop" puppet and children's *Learn to Sew Lace Up Cards* out of the bag. Eunice's tears began to flow once again down her cheeks and Moxie was at a loss for words.

As Moxie lifted the last item from the bag, Mildred said suddenly, "Eunice, where in the world did you dig this thing up? Where in God's name did you get it? I could have used it a long, long time ago. All three women cracked up laughing when they saw what Moxie had drawn out of the bag. The package held a "How to Hold onto Your Husband" apron which had do's and don'ts of married life printed across the fabric.

"What a wonderful hand-me-down!" said Moxie, laughing. "I might need it someday, if I find that certain special someone."

"I think you just have," Eunice said as she reached over and grabbed the rag doll and gently put it in Moxie's lap. You know what they say, "Truly great friends are hard to find, difficult to leave, and impossible to forget."

All three women stood at the same time, laughing, crying, giggling and doing all the things women of the heart do when they are together. They embraced tighter and longer than Moxie could remember ever being hugged before, along with Penelope, Moxie's long lost hand-sewn rag doll.

Acknowledgements

To my pre-publication readers, you know who you are and I appreciate your feedback. A special thanks to Kathy Shirley, Ph.D. who educated me on development of a fictional story. I loved how you helped me find the answers by asking the right questions. I am so grateful for your time and your expertise in consulting with me on this project.

Karen McLane of Postnet, you've read me well with each book cover you've created. I'm grateful to have worked with you once again.

Last but not least, heartfelt love and thanks to my husband, Terry, for his support and patience while I've pursued what has brought me great personal fulfillment—writing. And to my son, Marc, thanks for your technical knowledge and assistance with my official author website www.SowtheHeart.com.

About the Author

Sue Batton Leonard's first publication, a memoir, *Gift of a Lifetime: Finding Fulfilling Things in the Unexpected* won two EVVY Awards in the categories of anthology and audio books. It also won an award in the Young Adult category of the 2014 Harvest Book Competition.

Lessons of Heart and Soul, is an e-book of ten short stories cut from the manuscript of Gift of a Lifetime, and previously unpublished.

The beginnings of *Sew the Heart* came during the National Novel Writing Month 2014 as a personal challenge to write fiction.

Sue Batton Leonard is founder of Cornerstone Fulfillment Service, LLC and blog writer for www.SowtheHeart.com and www.allthingsfulfilling.com.

CPSIA information can be obtained
at www.ICGtesting.com
Printed in the USA
JSHW020238180922
30571JS00003B/140

9 781943 650347